BARUCH'S
— TALE —

The Story of the Prophet Jeremiah
Told by His Scribe

JOHN GIBBON

STONE TOWER PRESS

Stone Tower Press
7 Ellen Rd.
Middletown, RI 02842
stonetowerpress.com

Paperback ISBN: 978-1-7345859-4-0

Formatting and cover design by Amy Cole, JPL Design Solutions

Cover art: Rembrandt, "Jeremiah Lamenting the Destruction of Jerusalem" (1630) Oil on Canvas. Rijksmuseum, Amsterdam, Netherlands. Public Domain.

The ESV® Bible (The Holy Bible, English Standard Version®), copyright © 2001 by Crossway, a publishing ministry of Good News Publishers. Used by permission. All rights reserved.

Printed in the United States of America

"Thus says the LORD, the God of Israel, to you, O Baruch: You said, 'Woe is me! For the LORD has added sorrow to my pain. I am weary with my groaning, and I find no rest.' Behold, what I have built I am breaking down, and what I have planted I am plucking up – that is, the whole land. And do you seek great things for yourself? Seek them not, for behold, I am bringing disaster upon all flesh, declares the LORD. But I will give you your life as a prize of war in all places to which you may go."

Jeremiah 45:2-5

CONTENTS

AUTHOR'S PREFACE

The Babylonian siege of Jerusalem in 587 BCE,[1] resulting in the destruction of the city and Solomon's Temple, was a cataclysm that seared the history of Israel with burns whose scars show even today. The subsequent Babylonian Exile left permanent indentations on the contours of the history of the Middle East. The prophet Jeremiah stands out as the supreme figure in the events surrounding this tragedy of tragedies, yet even among those who are biblically well-read, the book that bears his name has a reputation for being one that is happily skipped over for something more palatable. Its uncompromising tone and lack of chronological order means that readers, educated in the modern media era, usually prefer the grand tragi-comedic opera played out by Daniel and King Nebuchadnezzar on the parallel but wider stage of the city of Babylon.

However, two other characters, central to the events in Jerusalem, appear as mere shadows on the fringe of the biblical account. The first was Jeremiah's secretary, Baruch the scribe, to whom he dictated his prophecies. The second was Nebuzaradan, captain of the Babylonian Royal Guard, who was in charge of the destruction of the Temple, the city walls and the subsequent deportation of the remnant of the population. The story begins one night in a room in a Babylonian palace where Baruch and Nebuzaradan, as very old men, recount their story

---

1   Of the two conventions generally in use (BC/AD or BCE/CE) I have opted for the latter.

to the elders of the community of exiles from the Kingdom of Judah.[2] There they tell of the events leading up to the Great Siege, its tragic consequences, and unfold their experiences afterwards. Even though he briefly appears as a biblical character, Nebuzaradan's history is my own invention, as are the boyhood histories of Jeremiah and Baruch. The boy Boaz, with whom we travel through the later part of the story, is an entirely fictional character. There is much that is not understood about Exilic and pre-Exilic practices so I hope rigorous biblical scholars will forgive my poetic licence in the way I have re-imagined certain scenes and events.

Together with its sister book of Lamentations, the book of Jeremiah tells the tragic story of a nation that had rejected its own history and had lost its way. It is also the personal story of a man of tender conscience and emotions who had been given the painful task of calling that nation back to its roots. The national crisis that unfolded over a generation ultimately ended in a destructive confrontation with a predatory foreign empire ruled by a dangerously unstable king who eradicated Jerusalem from the map and drove the surviving remnant of the population of Judah into captivity.

On a more personal level, why would an elderly British Gentile wish to write a historical novel of this type? A forty-seven-year fascination with the book of Jeremiah is one answer. In addition to this, the story of the Exile has lessons to teach anyone with an ear to listen, despite the fact that its message runs counter to the prevailing 21st-century secular cultural wind with its fashionable obsessions and ultra-sensitivities. It is regrettable that this wind carries with it a whiff of the anti-semitism which has again begun to flourish on both wings of the western political spectrum where age-old tropes and conspiracy theories have become the standard currency of social media. In a world where truth and lies mingle in a bewildering hall of mirrors, historical events can easily and deliberately be twisted out

---

2   In the text the people of Judah are called Judahites, just as the people of Israel were called Israelites. The name Judaea (Judea) did not come into use until later times.

of shape to suit hostile political agendas.³ At the back of the story of the Exile looms the exceedingly strange and dangerous figure of King Nebuchadnezzar of Babylon whose gross folly at trying to supplant the God of Heaven brought forth the stinging rebuke from the prophet Daniel:

> ... that the living may know that the Most High rules the kingdom of men and gives it to whom he will and sets over it the lowliest of men. (Dan 4:17)

Modern Nebuchadnezzar-like political activists and techno-visionaries who aim to 'change the world' should take note.

It would be extremely difficult to tell this story through the ancient Babylonian or Hebrew cultural mind, so I have tried to avoid a detailed immersion in the minutiae of dates, times, differences in calendars, customs and practices which would entangle the reader in awkward explanations without adding to the story. Instead, I have tried to tell it naturally in a way a modern reader would understand, using ideas and allusions familiar to this generation. Nevertheless, I have tried to pin various parts of it to a modern translation of the Bible (ESV) by the use of references. It is reasonable to assume that Baruch the scribe was raised in the old oral tradition of Scriptural memorization and would therefore have recalled all the words that Jeremiah dictated to him. Interweaving selected passages of the Books of Jeremiah, Lamentations and others into the story is deliberate. Even in an English translation, the lovely cadences of the variation and repetition of Hebrew poetry can often mask the tragedy described in the content. This novel is my way of re-telling Jeremiah's story without violating the scriptural narrative. The divinely inspired words of Scripture have a power and an elegance that mere secondary explanation does not. They do not just belong to that time alone but

---

3   The events of the Babylonian Exile are easily conflated with those belonging to 70 CE when Jerusalem and the Second Temple were besieged and destroyed by the Roman army, and an even later military campaign exiled Israel into her Diaspora after the Bar Kokhba Revolt of 135 CE.

speak to every generation and culture, so I believe it is best to let them tell their own story.

Inevitably, no project such as this can proceed without the generous help of others. My wife, Sheila, displayed great patience during the many iterations needed to turn this into a finished book, while she bolstered my flagging spirits and checked my text. Our close friend, the late, great Dr Anne Hinsley of Kingston-upon-Thames (Surrey), constructively commented on a very early version, while Rich Robinson of San Francisco and John Fenton of Bowdon Vale (Manchester) made some very helpful comments on a later version. However, my greatest thanks must go to Laurence Durston-Smith of Keswick (Cumbria) and Timothy Demy of Stone Tower Press, whose detailed and eagle-eyed critical reading produced a long list of invaluable constructive suggestions and corrections. To all of them I owe great thanks. Of course, all errors, both factual and typographical, are my own.

John Gibbon
London 2020

HISTORICAL TIME-LINE

Date BCE	Historical Time-Line
1010-970	Reign of David, first as King of Judah and then as King of all Israel.
970-930	Reign of Solomon, King of all Israel.
722	After defeat by Assyria, the northern Kingdom of Israel, based on Samaria, ceased to be an entity.
715-687	Reign of Hezekiah King of Judah who shut the gates of Jerusalem and defied Sennacherib King of Assyria.
687-642	Reign of Manasseh King of Judah.
642-640	Reign of Amon King of Judah.
640	Jeremiah, son of Hilkiah the priest, was born in Anathoth, a village just north east of Jerusalem. Josiah ascended the throne of Judah.
626	The call of Jeremiah and the death of Ashurbanipal King of Assyria. Nabopolassar, Governor of Babylon (626-605), rebelled against Assyria and became Babylon's King.

621	Religious Reformation in Judah began under Josiah (2 Kgs. 23:3). The book of the Law was found. Huldah the prophetess was consulted by Josiah (2 Kgs. 22:14). Jeremiah was commanded to reveal the contents of this covenant publicly (Jer. 11:1-8).
614	An alliance of Babylonians and Medes reduced Ashur and other strong-points in the Assyrian Empire. This alliance finally defeated the Assyrian Empire and destroyed the city of Nineveh in 612.
609	Josiah was killed in battle at Megiddo confronting Pharaoh Necho who was advancing to the aid of the Assyrians. Jehoahaz (4th son of Josiah) ascended the throne of Judah but Necho deposed him after 3 months in favour of his brother, the 2nd son Jehoiakim (Eliakim). Necho fined Judah a talent of gold and 100 talents of silver (2 Kgs. 23:31). Jehoiakim vacillated between Egypt and Babylon. His religious inclinations were idolatrous so he had little time for Jeremiah and his message (Jer. 26:20; 9:26).
609	In his Temple Address Jeremiah castigated the people for their superstitious trust in the Temple (Jer. 7:1-8; 12). He announced that it would be destroyed, thereby provoking public anger. His earlier experience at Anathoth was thus repeated (Jer. 11:18-23).
606	The first deportation: Daniel and others were taken to Babylon by Nebuchadnezzar.

605	Pharoah Necho marched his army to the River Euphrates but Crown Prince Nebuchadnezzar moved his own army from Haran and defeated the Egyptian army at Carchemish. Judah became a Babylonian tributary.
605	Nabopolassar, King of Babylon, died and Crown Prince Nebuchadnezzar became King.
600	Jehoiakim rebelled in a bid for independence despite Jeremiah's warnings regarding the outcome (Jer. 22:18).
598/7	The Babylonian Army invaded Judah and captured Jehoiakim who died before his deportation. He was succeeded by his son Jehoiachin (Jeconiah or Coniah) who initially shut the gates of Jerusalem against Nebuchadnezzar's army but then surrendered after three months. He was taken captive to Babylon, together with many skilled workmen (second deportation). Zedekiah (Mattaniah, Jehoiachin's uncle) was placed on the throne by Nebuchadnezzar as a puppet ruler (2 Kgs. 24:17).
589/88	Despite warnings from Jeremiah (Jer. 37:6, 38:1), a weak and vacillating Zedekiah was unable to prevent intrigue with Egypt among the ruling class who constantly urged rebellion in alliance with the new Egyptian Pharaoh Hophra. The Babylonian army invaded Judah in December 589 and besieged Jerusalem throughout the year 588 and into the year 587. Judah was urged to surrender by Jeremiah (Jer. 21:1; 34:1; 37:3; 38:1).

587	Jeremiah and Baruch attempted to leave the city, but were imprisoned, even though Zedekiah sought the advice of the prophet. The city fell in the mid-summer of the year 587, and was then pillaged. Zedekiah and all the leaders were captured and executed by Nebuchadnezzar. The Temple was burned and the city walls demolished. The third deportation to Babylon occurred. (There are two opposing views: the first holds that the Siege was 18 months in length, thereby ending in 587; the second holds that it was 30 months in length, thereby ending in 586. The author has adopted the first position.)
587	Jeremiah and Baruch released by Nebuzaradan and treated with respect. He appointed Gedaliah as Governor of Judah, who was joined by Jeremiah at Mizpah (Jer. 40:1). After the murder of Gedaliah, the Judahite remnant fled to Egypt, forcibly taking Jeremiah and Baruch with them (Jer. 42:1). Jeremiah passed his last days at Tahpanhes, together with Baruch, where he prophesied the ultimate defeat of Egypt by Nebuchadnezzar (Jer. 43:8).
571	Nebuchadnezzar and his Babylonian army invade Egypt.
562	Death of Nebuchadnezzar. Jechoniah released from prison in Babylon and given a place of honour at court.
550	Cyrus of Anshan (in Persia) conquered his Median overlord Astyages and then proceeded to conquer Lydia.
540	Cyrus conquered the Elamite Empire.

539	Cyrus defeated the Babylonian army at the battle of Opis on the River Tigris and entered the city of Babylon unopposed.
538-537	Cyrus issued a declaration that allowed subject peoples to return to their lands (Ez 1:1-4). Thus ended the Captivity.
537	First return of Exiles from Babylon to Jerusalem.
536	First attempt at rebuilding the new Temple.
536-530	The Temple rebuilding halted by an edict from the King of Persia.
520	The Temple rebuilding resumes after an appeal to the King.
516	The inauguration of the new Temple in Jerusalem.

1

AN ORPHAN OF
THE CAPTIVITY

The city of Babylon, "The Destroyer of Nations," has a name that causes a dark shadow to fall like a ragged curtain across the sunlight. What has been written of her that does not evoke fear and loathing and send a shudder down the spine of all the surrounding nations? She shall ever be called the accursed city, the mother of all evil, where rebellion against the God of Heaven was first attempted.

Our story began in this city one early morning in the summer of the year 550 BCE as the rising sun glowed on the edge of the horizon. Lazy and content in her dominance, the city lay astride the great River Euphrates as a reptile sprawls over its kill. The boy, whose name was Boaz, was waiting just outside the side-gate for the Market of the Fruit Vendors to open. Others had begun to move earlier, or had never slept. A vast shuffling army was already on the move. Flowing like a river in flood to the horizon, the encampments outside the city walls near the river-docks had disgorged armies of shackled slaves and captured prisoners moving like locust swarms feeding on the spring crop. The young and healthy were sold at market prices to work in the houses or labour on the estates of the wealthy. Others were merely

fodder sent out to die quickly in the heat and dust of the stone quarries and sun-drying brick kilns spread across her empire that fed the
ever-growing city. Babylon had winnowed the nations from the Nile
to the Euphrates and beyond. In the storm of her coming, their chaff
had been discarded to die in exhaustion and hunger.

One by one the cities of the nations had fallen to her sword. The
educated young males of the wealthy and the merchant classes had
been deported back to Babylon to be trained as clerks, secretaries,
translators, and even teachers, to serve the bureaucratic machine. The
young women were taken as slave girls to be used or discarded at will
in the houses and pagan temples. Only a few lived to reach a dignified
middle age. The old were left to die around the many ruined walls of
the conquered cities of the surrounding nations. Of those deported,
the weak soon died and the hardy were the only ones who reached this
city alive.

Babylon destroyed any nation that resisted her will, while simultaneously salvaging its talent to be put to its own use. It was a meat-
grinding machine, feeding on the wealth of nations and growing ever
fatter. Now the largest city in the world she left a deserted wasteland
of her conquered neighbours.

Boaz stood both fascinated and horrified as the daily grind of
the wheels and blades of this machine whirred in motion before his
eyes. The survivors staggered half-dead from the slave-ships at the
wharves, and were then marched out to the camps to be processed.
Having been born into this city meant its motions and odours were
no surprise to him, but fear still gripped his heart as he surveyed
the sight before him. None of his people could forget that they were
merely a remnant that had been spared the meat grinder that he saw
in operation before him. This could have been his fate, or might still
be if he made a mistake or was just unlucky.

As his name would suggest, he was a descendant of the remnant from Judah which had been deported before the destruction
of Jerusalem a generation before. The deepest and most dangerous
thoughts of this remnant were never to be expressed in public, but
if they were written in the sky in bold letters they would spell out

"Babylon, the destroyer of the Temple, and the leveller of the walls of Jerusalem." She would never be forgotten nor forgiven for all generations.

Whatever lay deep within his subconscious mind, Boaz was no different from any other young man roused from his precious bed too early for his growing teenage body, and commanded by his elders to fulfill his allotted duty. The transport of the regular fruit order – plums, melons, prunes, dates, citron – was not an arduous duty. Nevertheless, his long, awkward teenage body made a rather comical sight, like an ant pushing its burden back to the nest. His sleepy morning feeling was quickly dispelled by the effort of trundling the heavy cart and within him awoke the voracious breakfast hunger that only the young experience.

Suddenly a traffic jam of tangled carts and people appeared in the narrow streets ahead of him. He had been taught the wisdom of being careful not to provoke others by a show of aggression in such circumstances. An empty, noisy shouting match could turn to personal violence, which might escalate into mob violence against his people. For a triviality like this, too many had been shipped off as slaves to die miserable early deaths in the quarries. All that for a few minutes delay.

"Stay quiet boy, and learn patience," a gentle, kindly elder had once whispered in his ear. "One day your time to speak will come."

He waited and waited and mused on the city itself. Across the river lay some of its great sights, such as the Etemenanki Ziggurat, its elaborate gardens and some of its eight gates. Among the more pious Judahites there were parts of the city that were forbidden, for the simple reason that they were associated with the Babylonian idol religions and the worship of their master-god Marduk. In their own eyes, the citizens of Babylon saw their city as the centre of the world and a symbol of the cosmic harmony that had come into existence when Marduk defeated the forces of chaos. The pious among the exiles saw this paradise on earth very differently. It had been impressed upon those willing to listen that the hundreds of pagan temples and shrines that littered the street corners were little more than prostitution shops, served by bevies of sad slave girls and boys who were forced to serve their clientele in the name of some idol deity. Sickness, disease or just plain grief made an end of most of them before they were hardly out of their teenage years. "Keep away boy, do not go there" had been the whispered injunction. Unlike other boys, whose curiosity would have been aroused, it had always been the famed, enormous, thick walls that had fascinated him. He did not ask, as others did, "How can men build such things?" for he knew that tens of thousands of slaves, including many of his own people, had died labouring in the quarries and hauling the huge stones that now sat so benignly in serried rows.

"If those stones could talk, what stories would they tell?" He then dismissed this as a thought unworthy of everything he had been taught. It was absurd to ask if stones could talk. The nations had laboured and exhausted themselves to build a wall made from objects that never moved, yet many in this city went to temples and prayed to gods carved of the same stone. The Babylonians believed themselves to be tormented by the ghosts and evil spirits of men who had experienced unhappy lives or who had suffered violent death. These spirits haunted their dream-world, or so they thought, which caused them to part with hard-won gold while fervently asking for protection or elaborate favours from the pantheon of idol-gods in those same temples.

Boaz had been taught rigorously, but furtively, that such crude pagan beliefs and forms of worship were forbidden to his people. He had even heard stories that they were in this very city because their own fathers had once indulged in such forbidden practices, but it was talked of only in whispers.

The trail of wagons in front of him moved suddenly, waking him from his reverie. Half an hour more saw him guide his load through the side-streets along the pathways by the wall, trodden mainly by the servants and slaves of the houses. This way, he knew, led back to the Residence and food. That is not what they called it in Hebrew but as an anonymous public name it did well enough not to draw attention to its function.

Few of the residents ever wondered how it was that their commune survived the struggles, riots, and sporadic violence that erupted in the city, provoked by the princely factions that rose and fell over the years. The royal princes of Babylon, the descendants of the younger brothers of the now deceased Nebuchadnezzar, were many. Known for their rapacity, they fed off the plundered wealth and talent of the nations, taking their share and much more besides. Few survived who resisted their will. The great merchant families of all origins who had grown from nothing, rising on their skill in money-making in markets of plundered goods, or even in simple everyday food and fruit, had to pay protection money to survive.

Boaz had only recently become conscious of how tenuous was the life of any merchant family. His close friend Mordecai had recently disappeared when the great Persian merchant Teresh, for whom he worked as a secretary and clerk, had lost his business. Overnight it had been shut down and its houses and goods had been sequestered by a faction of soldiers under the orders of a Babylonian prince. The merchant family had disappeared overnight, as had his friend. To ask after Mordecai was futile. No-one would know except, perhaps, an anonymous slave-secretary who made out the lists of those that had been sold. It was also dangerous to inquire, for there would be those whose malignant curiosity would be aroused over his questioning which might make him a marked man. Clandestine gossip said that the protection money old Teresh had paid was not enough and negotiations had become too slow. None was exempt when a great prince in the city was desperate for money, and it was money that slipped through their blood-stained hands like water.

The Residence was a long, low-slung building that backed against the city walls. Superficially it looked like an unobtrusive warehouse or barracks, giving it the air of a giant lean-to shack. The few windows that existed at street level had stout wooden bars to discourage thievery and the inquisitive. Its anonymous visage said that it was content to remain so, with stores and workmen dribbling in and out of its lesser doors. The interior revealed a series of levels that went deep underground, all of which backed onto the city wall whose huge stones kept it cool in the summer heat, particularly in the afternoon. The floors were supported by large, horizontal wooden beams embedded in the wall at one end and the frontage at the other, with the main weight being taken by vertical wooden posts. The frontage itself was built of layers of typical Babylonian mud-brick sealed together with bitumen. Openings in the front wall at various upper levels captured the breeze and allowed the air to vent, which was an absolute necessity, given the heat and the number of people it housed. To Boaz, it was just home – the boys, the girls and the old men and women living on separate floors. He had no real memory of anywhere else. The vast interior, so much more capacious than its outer appearance, smelled overpoweringly of olive oil that permeated everything. In the twilight of the lower levels the oil lamps burnt round the clock leaving even the stones with an oily feel.

It functioned as an orphanage, school, hospital and a wayside home. Of his father no trace remained, if it had ever existed. Only soft, faint childhood recollections of his mother occasionally stirred his subconscious. None spoke of them for there was nothing to say. The wholesale genocides of the last half-century, mingled with fever epidemics that had carried off even more, had sliced into ancestral and community memories, leaving only survivors with a forgotten past and a precarious future. All that Boaz knew was that his ancestors belonged to the two groups exiled before the Great Siege of Jerusalem.[4] More than fifty years before his time, the Babylonian army had moved swiftly westwards and had defeated Egypt in a great battle at Carchemish[5] in a bend of the River Euphrates. Many battles are irrelevancies in the great scheme of things but Carchemish was a hinge on which had turned a great page of history. From that point Babylon had become the new great power in the region, flexing her muscles and demanding both financial and cultural tribute from all the surrounding nations, even from those beyond the River. The little Kingdom of Judah had been one of these, which is why the great Daniel had arrived in Babylon as a very young man. From this human tribute, which was just another name for a set of hostages, a select

4   587 BCE.

5   605 BCE.

group of young men had been chosen to be trained and indoctrinated into Babylonian ways. This was the first deportation. The plan had been to show their own people back home how things were going be done in future. Eight years later, the Babylonian army had captured Jerusalem[6] after a three-month-long resistance, driving off the ever-meddling Egyptians in an easily won action, after which a second and much bigger set of deportees had been demanded and had arrived in the city of Babylon. Accompanying them was their new King, an eighteen year old Jehoiachin, with his foolish, fawning uncle Zedekiah replacing him as a puppet on the Judahite throne. The thousands of these second exiles had included many skilled craftsmen and smiths. Not only were people exiled to Babylon but also the vessels of the Jerusalem Temple. Ten disastrous years later, the rebellion against Babylonian rule, and the subsequent Great Siege, had produced a third ragged set of deportees, emaciated and exhausted. Few had survived the journey and even fewer had lived long enough to put down roots. They had trusted in Egypt yet again to no avail. Nebuchadnezzar had flown into manic fury at being defied which had resulted in the eradication of the Temple, the city of Jerusalem and the Kingdom of Judah – nothing after it would ever be the same again. This catastrophe had also turned the Judahite exiles in Babylon itself into a potentially treasonable element, forever under suspicion. It was thus a miracle that a remnant of their people had survived. Other neighbouring nations had just disappeared in the deluge of the Babylonian storm. It was from within the more pious Judahite survivors that a desperate and despairing craving grew to return to their land and rebuild.

Of the Judahite people in Babylon, only their royal family, who now had some status at the Babylonian royal court, and a few thousand families of the first and second deportations could reliably trace their lineage back in the history of Judah. For the rest, the Great Siege itself lay like a great jagged chasm, cleaving through and eradicating their history leaving an orphaned generation in its wake. As one of these children of the captivity, Boaz had been placed in the Residence by a kindly, anonymous hand. All he had been told was that his

6   597 BCE.

family had been of Levitical descent. Perhaps he had been a large baby because his name in Hebrew meant `strength is within him'. Not only was it the name of the great grandfather of King David who had married Ruth the Moabitess, it was also the name of one of two bronze pillars, eighteen cubits high, which had once supported the porch of the now demolished Jerusalem Temple built by King Solomon.[7] Indeed Boaz was well-named for he was tall, akin to a pillar, and still growing rapidly.

The Residence also doubled over as a rest home for the elderly, but now increasingly a terminal hospital. Of the details of the history of the Residence no record had ever been written and never would: it was just there, and had been before his birth. The few who had survived to reach a full age were now at the dying age and it was here they saw their last hours. Boaz had noticed how the old lived more in the past than the present. He was always amused when one of them would begin a sentence with the words "I remember ...." for then it would be followed by interminable recollections, but for many of that generation the memories were what they wished to forget but never could. In the old days tradition dictated that Boaz would have lived in a Levitical community with all its necessary rituals and observances. That life had been destroyed beyond imagining. Boaz was simply a random brand plucked from the fire, or so he thought, a survivor mixed in with the rest. The crushing and dismemberment of a nation could not have been more complete.

From day to day the exiles survived as best they could. Some worked for, and were looked after, by the older families who themselves had to pay protection money to stay safe. Their futures, particularly the merchants, rose and fell with the fluctuating political fortunes of the times. At best, survival was precarious. Others were slaves of the great houses and estates spread across the empire, doing the bidding of their masters day by day. For them, nothing could be done, but the Residence itself was there to shelter those who fell outside these networks within and around the city. This pattern was replicated all around the empire. To the young, only semi-conscious of

7   2 Chron. 3:17.

their own tattered history, it was just their home, and a place for food to assuage their constant hunger. Strangely, it never occurred to them to ask who paid the bills.

As each day passed they thanked the Lord God of Israel for one more day of peace. Any refugee survivor group was ripe for plunder and the Judahites were always the first on every list. Babylon was a pot seething with people, from whom recruitment by the princes into one of their private, half-trained, ill-disciplined militias was easy. Once the great Daniel had retired, the usurpation of his powers had given encouragement to their enemies. Each day they waited apprehensively for the heavy mob of one or another of these princely militias to pour in through the doors, taking axes to the wooden window bars, stripping everything, leaving only wreckage, even though they owned nothing of value. The old and alert watched and wondered in bewilderment how their Residential haven of peace could survive, but survive it did. The trouble milling round the streets always seemed to miraculously stop short of them.

At the back of the building, in the low, constant, twilight near the base of the city wall, was the part assigned to the old. Here they expired gently, alone with their sad memories, and nursed their grief in silence. Despite the coolness of the stones, it was not necessarily the best place for them because this deeper part suffered from dampness during high-river periods after heavy rains in the far-off mountains of Cappadocia in the north western part of the Median Empire. A few, a very few, of the old were mobile, and these would wander around the building, snoozing away the day curled on one of the many rush mats that littered the place. One of these old men Boaz actually knew, at least by sight. Some days this old man had an ancient look with wrinkles deep like rock crevices, shuffling along with a stoop. On other days he looked forty years younger with a smoother skin and an upright bearing. How old was he? Boaz did not know nor did he even think to ask the question, for he was of an age when anyone of the next generation looked old to him. The great Daniel was now very old, he knew, but how old was beyond him. Anyway, the whispers said that

Daniel lived in retirement, protected, unseen by the envious, vengeful, prying eyes of the princes.

"How was the fruit market today, boy?" asked the old man. "It's Boaz, is it not?"

"Yes sir, my name is Boaz," he replied listlessly. He had still not quite emerged from the attitude of automatic sullenness, deference and denial that schoolboys of every age have adopted to adults around them. "The market was the same as ever, sir, but I never stay long. The order is pre-arranged and I am just the collector."

"Ah, quite so," said the old man in a low voice, "it is wise to avoid getting close to those slave-trains and the poor creatures in the lines." Then, in a muttered aside, he said "I once knew how it was – too well. Those lines were like the Nile in flood. You should have seen it – like rivers to the horizon."

"The Nile, sir? Is that not in Egypt? I have only heard of Egypt. It is said that none of our people living there ever survived to come here after ...." He hesitated, and then said "after the King ...." His voice trailed away into silence, for he knew he was speaking of only fourth and fifth hand tales, distorted by the legends that always grew with the telling. Who knew what was true? Whenever these were raised, an elder quickly quashed any talk. Talk like that was dangerous, for it could be maliciously interpreted as the beginning of a conspiracy.

He assumed the conversation was over. The young always thought that their polite, puzzled exchanges with the old were about ancient memories, the things of long ago tangled in a web they were unable to unpick. This community was different, for their memories of long ago made people shudder and reduced them to silence. The young soon learned not to ask too many questions and he knew he was treading on difficult ground.

Boaz turned away in his embarrassment but suddenly the old man spoke again.

"Yes, Egypt, a place I once knew but never will again ... darkness," he muttered and then fell silent. He suddenly shrank into his skin, like an old man, and looked a thousand years old. "Stick to this place, boy. Do not get a craving to wander the earth, as young men do. This is not a time to see the world, for the world has come to you in this city. You have friends here, more than you know. Unknown hands here, even in Babylon, have been sent from on high, that will protect you."

Then, with a cheerfully dismissive wave of the hand, he said "Never mind me, boy. Take no notice of my rambling," and wandered off.

There was vague rustling among the floor-rushes as if someone had been listening and had scurried off. No event, not even a whispered conversation in such a place, was ever really private and wicked talk said that some here had been bribed or blackmailed to report back to the authorities.

Boaz thought nothing of this as his mind was distracted by his amusement at the words of the old man. Do the old always talk like this in vague aphorisms, kindly meant, that lack any practical meaning or sense, all based on past memories? Even so, the mention of Egypt remained with him. It was said that many who had fled down to Egypt from the ruins of Jerusalem after the Great Siege had been lost, including the fabled prophet Jeremiah and his secretary Baruch the scribe. Later on, the wholesale slaughter in the wake of the harrying of Egypt by King Nebuchadnezzar had accounted for even more. Dark rumours said that none of the Judahite remnant had ever come to Babylon by way of Egypt. If this was so, how did the old man speak of Egypt in this manner? He tried to dismiss the thought.

It was time to eat with the rest of his group at the rough tables made of planks and bench-like seating. Boys of his age were always noisy and irrepressibly boisterous, consuming good barley flatbread and vegetables like wolves. For the older boys there was also diluted barley-beer, the local brew. The cry "Not too much, not too much" was in his head. The matriarch Deborah, who ruled over them, made sure of that. She could freeze you with a look and strike terror into even the stoutest of the older men but she was genuinely kindly and could not hide it. Moreover, everyone knew it, which diminished its effectiveness. Malingerers were dealt with by a smack of the back of her hand but the genuinely ill were looked after as if they were a son. He felt lucky, for she seemed to like Boaz. She knew he was a gentle boy, cut out more for the life of a secretary or scholar than as hired muscle.

His mind came back to the wine barrels he had recently seen loaded at one of the merchant houses. Babylonians did not usually drink wine but those who had conquered and visited other nations had learned to like it. Someone had once told him that the wines of Sibnah in Moab had been the most coveted. The Residence had occasionally been given the odd barrel or two, but of ever changing variety. It appeared at odd times, sent by cart from one of the sympathetic merchant houses, spare barrels shipped off the sleek, gliding ships on the great River coming from somewhere, going anywhere. Who knows which set of vineyards had been plundered by the great and then their barrels sold for silver, ending in the cellars of one of the great houses whose trading arms littered the river bank. The Residence was content to accept the left-overs, the spare barrels nobody else wanted, for then no offence was given and they could go on living in the shadows. Only the old asked for how long.

Yes, the wine again: how many times in their lessons had those passages in Proverbs on not drinking too much wine been force-fed into them? Boaz had been taught the language and content of the Scriptures of his people since childhood. The elegance of Hebrew lived within him but the practicalities of street life meant using Aramaic, the language of the street and the bustling markets. He was currently being trained with a view to becoming a scribe, a fledgling teacher of the Law of Moses, of the old prophets and of the wisdom literature of his people. His elders had planned this for him and this was what he wanted too. Would it work out? Much depended upon the necessary financial support being available over many years. A more likely route would be for him to end up as a secretary or man of business in a merchant trading house. That would mean dealing in the trade and politics of the city. He was not the sort of personality to be consumed by ambition or anxiety.

Despite the failings of their fathers and the catastrophe that had befallen them, did all Judahites care about their ancestral history? Some were happy to live in the Babylonian way and gave no thought to their ancestral traditions, but for the pious remnant who were trying to walk in the ancient paths, survival in the seething Babylonian melting-pot meant a precarious balance between a rigorous separation from the local pagan rituals of daily life, and assimilation into its ways. To their enemies, the separatists stood out as obvious targets, while even the assimilated could be suspected of undermining the existing order simply by being assimilated. Despite these contradictions, it had been impressed upon Boaz that silent absorption and neutral conformity was the way to pass unnoticed. His most influential teacher, the scribe Itamar, had taught him that a successful military commander began by trying to understand how his opponents thought. What influences them? What moves them and drives them? Get inside their head to know what move they will make in this great and deadly game before they know it themselves. To do this in Hebrew meant peering through a fog. To do it in Aramaic meant you had already breached their walls. He could think and speak in either language without any conscious switch. For an innocent young man like Boaz, such was the daily balancing act. What of the great dreams that reside in the eye of the mind of every teenage boy? The great soldier, standing proudly victorious on the field of battle? Riches beyond avarice? Women? Boaz had no such dreams, or, if he did, they came only in a kaleidoscopic flicker, to be quickly extinguished. Survival for a child of the Captivity meant living in the present, to get through the day, the next day, the next week, the next month. Next year could look after itself.

TWO OLD MEN
MEET AGAIN

The mere mention of the words "Nile" and "Egypt" were two pebbles that started a landslide. It began as a mere puff of dust, then a small slither of earth and stones, which seemed to be nothing until suddenly a crack opened in the side of the mountain. Then the earth suddenly slipped, slithered and skipped downhill, gathering momentum until the whole mountainside seemed to be on the move.

Boaz wandered out for a walk to clear his head after breakfast. Living inside the Residence could become overly oppressive, but entering the surrounding Babylonian street system was a guessing game. Potentially, a solitary person could always be picked on by roaming street criminals but his height not only made him stand out like a thin pine tree but also his teenage awkwardness and gentle-looking face made him a natural target for every bully looking for trouble. In the febrile atmosphere and the heat, even the seemingly greater safety of a group could escalate into a street riot. Among the many minorities in this part of the city, the Judahites were the usual victims, although some of them knew how to fight back and relished the prospect. Strangely, the Residence itself always emerged unscathed, seemingly immune from the street troubles around it.

Boaz was due for his long session with the scribe Itamar. He enjoyed these. Itamar was a kindly man who understood how a good, voracious, young mind could soak up information, but he also comprehended its limitations in grasping the bigger picture into which each slice of knowledge fitted, a picture that came only with age and experience. That gave him a sympathetic understanding of the young who responded to him in kind.

"What is it?" asked the scribe. "You seem troubled, and far away. You do not seem able to concentrate on the matter in hand."

"Oh, no sir, I am not really troubled but I confess that I am puzzled about something I heard earlier." He told him about his conversation with the old man. "So many stories have been told about those terrible times in Egypt, with no corroboration – that much I have learned from you – and then suddenly the old man mentioned it all so casually as if he had been there. I find it all so surprising. It cannot really be true, can it?"

The part about the Nile also puzzled Itamar who stored it away for later. Of this he gave no sign. Outwardly, to Boaz, he just shrugged it off by saying "Probably not, my boy, probably not. Old men occasionally have queer fancies, you know, and sometimes talk of things outside their experience. I believe it is of no consequence. Let us move on."

They did indeed move on, too rapidly today, for Boaz struggled to keep up. "Perhaps the scribe is distracted, like me, and has forgotten to slow down?" It never occurred to him that their distraction was over the same thing.

Later that night, the community elders met at an unobtrusive house with no name, a place across the city where they always met. The majority were scribes, associated with and supported by the bigger families and the royal family. Among them was Itamar, who had a longstanding reputation for probity in their community. He also represented those for whom the Residence catered. There were committees like this in every city over the empire where the Exiles were distributed.

The business was long but routine: who needed help, who was being awkward and what to do about various difficult situations. It was just the ways and means of a community on the edge trying to function. They were always careful. To publicly organize anything for the community benefit could be interpreted by enemies as a revolt against authority, and enemies they had in plenty.

In the break, when the refreshments went round, the talk flowed freely. The scribe Itamar spoke up, addressing Eleazar the chief scribe for the city and their chairman.

"I have a boy, Boaz, under my tutelage at the Residence, a good boy. You may remember him?"

Eleazar was always slow to respond. He was one of those who did not realise how long he took to think.

Finally he said "Yes, I do recall him. A boy worth educating, we have all agreed, and your efforts do not seem to have been in vain. We all have high hopes of him."

"He told me today about an old man at the Residence. You may know him, although he is very like most old men in our care. We call him Joseph. He seems ageless and anonymous. Maybe it was twenty years ago when he appeared – the usual nameless and anonymous history of the dispossessed – but that would not be unusual. He has always avoided talking about his past but it is what he said to Boaz earlier in the day that has puzzled both of us. He suddenly began to speak about Egypt, not in generalities, but in ways that implied he had been there. How could this be?"

Another younger scribe spoke up. "But that is impossible, he must be rambling." He seemed almost angry, indignant even. "Of the remnant that went down to Egypt after the Siege, no survivors ever came from there to Babylon. We were told that. It was definite. Old men ramble, they always do. There are some who would even accuse us here of that," he said with a chuckle, his usual good humour finally breaking through.

"What we have been told and what is actually true may not be the same," said Eleazar, "although I agree it is an unlikely story."

There was a timid knock on the door and an acutely nervous-looking servant whispered something into the ear of Eleazar who responded, "Here, in this house, now?"

Eleazar blanched white, and a nervousness suddenly infected him. "A senior officer from the House of the Captain of the Royal Guard is here and wishes to speak to us." To the servant he said "Show him in."

In walked the officer. Past experience dictated that he would swagger contemptuously and accuse them of some outlandish set of crimes and conspiracies -- the usual tactics of the bully to un-nerve the victim before the kill. Instead he stood respectfully and spoke quietly and politely to the chief scribe.

"Sir, I know it is late but my master requests your presence, all of you, at his private residence. Have no fear. Let me assure you that you are safe with me and my men. Moreover, my master is not whom you think, although you will have heard of him, I believe? He is Nebuzaradan, who is now an old, old man; it is his eldest son who is now Captain of the Royal Guard, but it is the elder Nebuzaradan who wishes to speak to you."

It was as if a storm had shaken the foundations of the room! Nebuzaradan, once the captain of the Royal Guard under King Nebuchadnezzar and one of a fabled generation who, long, long ago, had breached the Jerusalem city walls in the Great Siege. Later he had burnt the Temple, broken down the city walls and deported the people. Even the mention of his name struck fear into every Judahite heart, etched forever with grief. They had heard rumours that he was still alive, but Babylon was full of rumours, most untrue. So it *was* true, and he wished to speak with them. The storm of sudden emotion and fear blowing through the room had shaken their foundations and each man gasped inwardly as if bent double by a blow.

"He asks that three more attend the meeting," said the officer. "My master wishes the boy Boaz and the old man you call Joseph to be present. To avoid gossip would one of you go back to your

Residence and bring them here quietly and unobtrusively without talk? Then we may leave together. He also asks that the High Priest, Jozadak, be summoned."

Eleazar nodded to Itamar and whispered, "Yes, bring them here quietly with no fuss. There is clearly more to this than meets the eye." Then he asked one of the other members to summon Jozadak. The men left quietly.

To the officer he said "Sir, can we offer you something to drink while we wait? Please take a seat? What of your men, for we assume you have an escort?"

The polite niceties organized and over, Eleazar thought "At least there are some in Babylon with good manners, exquisite manners even."

Itamar returned soon with his two charges. He fussed over Boaz who was clearly fearful, while Joseph, the old man, looked alert and relaxed, even faintly amused. A military escort at night with a train of prisoners turned no heads in Babylon, although the more alert would have noticed that the escorted were walking freely with no signs of violence upon them. Quietly, confidently, they moved round to one side of the palace, through a series of doors and courtyards until they entered a medium-sized room, decorated tastefully with vases and silver ornaments. The quality of the chairs and tables shone out in contrast to the rough but durable benches and table-planks of the Residence.

"It will be in here," said the officer.

Servants arrived with a selection of the local barley-beer, wine they had never seen before, olives, and fruit. Normally they would have refused participation but tonight was not a night to argue over food. Then Jozadak the High Priest arrived to be greeted with solemn respect all round. He looked both puzzled and apprehensive.

"It may be a long night so I suggest you sit, and make yourselves comfortable," said the young officer.

A long night! They all wondered over the meaning of the term. Why were they here? One of the more junior members of the party, agitated and emotional, burst out with "But sir, what have we done?"

"Calm yourself, young one," said Jozadak. "Life is full of surprises and this is one of them, but we are in no danger here, I detect." The officer smiled in agreement. After a while, a shuffling outside the door indicated the presence of men moving and carrying something. In walked four men carrying a bed like a litter, which cleverly folded at the middle to turn into a chair, like a wicker throne. Its occupant was a very old man, dressed in a black cloak, who sat upright. His hair was white and swathed a face that commanded attention, with penetrating eyes that looked upon the world with stern amusement. It was clear that no-one trifled with such a man as this. He dismissed his carriers but commanded the young officer to remain.

"Let me introduce myself. My name is Nebuzaradan. My eldest son is now the official Captain of the Guard, but I am he of whom you have no doubt heard much," adding dryly, "I doubt that any of it was flattering."

The occupants of the room seemed frozen into silence, fascinated and horrified yet befuddled by the anticipation they felt.

"Yes, I can see that you would all naturally shrink back from the one who destroyed Jerusalem long ago, but I assure you I mean you no ill -- this time. Whispers have begun and it is time for an old story to unfold and you must hear it, for it concerns your people and it also concerns me. I have not invited your Royal Family as I wish to keep matters private. No doubt you will report to them in time but for the moment it is best they stay out of this."

"I assume you are Boaz?" turning to the boy. "Today, a little bird on the breeze told me of your conversation."

Turning back to the full group he continued to speak. "First, has it ever occurred to you to ask why your Residence has remained untouched by any of the unruly princes in this city?"

"We have indeed often wondered, my Lord," said Eleazar "why we have been left alone in peace. Was it under your orders? If so, we thank you."

"My officers here have let it be known among the princely mobs that no-one, but no-one, is to touch your Residence, upon pain of death. In the far past I did much to damage to your people but at least

I can claim this protection to my credit, and discreet financial support on your behalf. Let us say it is a small morsel in the balance of many, heavier, greater sins."

He turned to Boaz again. "In Babylon there are informers everywhere who report to men who wish you ill. Therefore, I too make it my business to know what has been said and what is being done in your house. That way I can better protect you. Your little talk today tinkled a few bells and the noise reached me this afternoon."

He took a small sip from his cup. "You must think that my manners have deserted me. Forgive me for not rising to greet you. My legs are not what they were, but there is one here I must greet as an old friend."

The room was puzzled. Old friend? Among us?

"Step forward, Joseph. It has been a long time." Joseph rose slowly, went forward and bowed deeply.

"My Lord, we indeed meet again. I see you have not lost your touch for the dramatic gesture! We are clearly in for an interesting night. The time has come, has it not? My indiscretion earlier today has made it inevitable. The story needs to be told and I have kept my secret too long." Each man seemed to attempt to out-twinkle the other as if they were friendly rivals in an old game.

"Joseph, as you call him, has been living among you for so long, that none of you have noticed him. That was our intention, as he wished to live in anonymity in rest and peace. I placed him among you and swore your original warden to secrecy, even though he never knew the real identity of Joseph. He died long ago and kept his word, so none of you ever knew how Joseph came to you."

There was an alertness about the room, a deathly silence. Each man was lost to their thoughts. Who could Joseph be? What was all this? After what seemed an age, Nebuzaradan said "I can sense your impatience. Time rewards old men with patience as she takes away other faculties."

There ensued a shuffling as each settled in for a long session. They had clearly not reached the patient stage yet.

"I thought of placing Joseph with your Daniel – yes, I know Daniel well and we are friends and allies – but while Daniel is protected, the princes have always had him watched like a hawk. His presence would have been noticed, so I placed him with you."

Another ageless silence ensued as each contemplated their thoughts. "The time has come to tell you who he really is and hear his story from his own lips – and mine. You are ready Joseph?"

Joseph bowed his assent. He seemed to be enjoying himself.

"Gentlemen," said Nebuzaradan, "let me introduce you to Baruch, son of Neriah – Baruch the scribe – otherwise known to you as Joseph."

The silence in the room was deafening. Each was lost to their vivid, whirling thoughts at the news. Baruch the scribe, the friend of the prophet Jeremiah and his secretary, who wrote down and ultimately read his prophecies aloud to Zedekiah the King when the prophet was imprisoned in Jerusalem at the height of the Great Siege.

It was on the face each man in the room. "But he must have been dead for an age, as long dead as Jeremiah had been dead, dead, dead… Jeremiah, who had died after his enforced flight to Egypt, accompanied by Baruch. Yes, Egypt!" Each man made the mental connection within seconds of each other. Baruch had miraculously survived and had been living among them for years, decades, in plain sight, and no-one knew. How could this be?

Baruch-Joseph looked calmly around at them. "Yes, I am indeed Baruch and I really am that old, as is my Lord Nebuzaradan here. We both belong to a different age and time. But hear me. Whatever, in your eyes, he once did, he found me, he has protected me, and he has protected you these last years. Grant him that much. If we reach a measure of peace in this room, the story we both have to tell will sit easier upon you. Indeed, it is as much his story as mine."

3

NEBUZARADAN'S TALE

After a short silence it was Nebuzaradan who began by turning to Boaz, "Young men find the tales of the old tedious, do they not? Yet this story began seventy years ago when I was just 20 years old – not much older than you."

Boaz smiled and shuffled, but his fascination was growing like an itch that demanded to be scratched.

"Can you believe that Baruch and I have shared ninety summers? Your prophet Jeremiah would have too, if he had lived. Is that not so, Baruch? The three of us of the same age are all part of this story."

Baruch nodded gently.

"There is also a fourth, slightly older than us and long since dead, who also figures, but I will tell you of him in good time if you can bear with the rambling memories of an old man. Meanwhile, let us begin at the beginning."

"I was a young officer in the army of the old king, Nabopolassar,[8] who began as the governor of our city in the days when this city was part of the old Assyrian empire. You would have had to travel for months in every direction across Assyria to reach its outer edges. It seemed to fill the whole earth. To give you some idea of how far it

---

8   Nabopolassar (658-605 BCE) was ruler of the neo-Babylonian empire (626-605 BCE).

reached, the city of Thebes in Egypt was conquered by Ashurbanipal, King of Assyria, more than a hundred years ago. He was an educated, polished and sophisticated man, but brutal to those who rebelled against him – just like us. Did you know that he also defeated and devastated Babylon in the rebellion about ten years before I was born? Babylon and Nineveh had always been old sparring partners with a history of wars that goes far back beyond our time."

"Finally the Assyrian Empire grew too large and cumbersome. The constant demand for troops to quell every local rebellion became so expensive that it ground to a halt and ran out of money. Rebellions are always about taxes. It is the classic circular problem. The demand for taxes from his cities and provinces grew ever greater and with these the rebellions grew more frequent. The usual punishment was to devastate a rebellious vassal, as Ashurbanipal did to Elam, but the problem with that strategy is that wasted kingdoms are never capable of paying taxes, while costing a fortune to suppress."

"There came a time when our governor, Nabopolassar, simply refused to comply. He was an energetic, forceful man who was also an excellent organizer. He finally decided that we had to go our own way, but to do this required more than just breaking away. The Assyrian Empire would never lie down quietly and let us go. If it was to be done, it would be a fight to the death and would eventually require the conquest of Nineveh itself. We understood that and planned for it right from the beginning. The righteous zeal and fury of the oppressed was enough to drive us onward to victory over Nineveh. But then we had real leaders and an army hungry for their rewards. Once they tasted the fruits of victory they cast envious eyes over neighbours whose gold and silver dazzled their eyes. When does one stop? When is enough ever enough? We could not stop. That is why we have grown from being a subject people into the devouring monster, the Destroyer of Nations, you see today."

"Nevertheless, in those early days, Nabopolassar was not only a great planner, but he also had immense patience. He had it all worked out long before. He foresaw that this would be the work of a lifetime. His best and most radical idea began much earlier, but came to fruition when the final momentous decision was made. It was to gather private information on what his enemies were thinking and planning long before the breakaway was made. In other words, he set out to build an intelligence service. It does not seem very exciting when told in this way. It is easy, too easy, to send out a few merchants in a camel-train to surreptitiously count enemy troops, or for a general to send out patrols to determine the dispositions of his enemy. Anyone can play that sort of game, and everyone does it. He wanted more, much more. He understood from the beginning that not only did we need real inside information on the plans and disposition of our enemies, but also on those that might become enemies in the far future."

"For this we needed a bird listening in every palace chamber to discover how its occupants thought, what plans they had, how strong they were financially and militarily and, more important than any of these, the state of their morale. He wanted to know in advance when even a mouse changed rooms. He knew that a rebellious people with a set of foolish, intriguing, drunken leaders are already half-way to defeat. To have this information in detail in advance of a campaign is an immense advantage. Moreover, he wanted this in every major city across the empire, not just Nineveh, but as far as Damascus, Tyre, Susa and even Jerusalem. It sounds dull and unromantic – unlike the flashing swords and noise of the battle so attractive to young men – but it is very effective and saves innumerable lives and mistakes."

"These cities may not have been enemies at that time, as Judah was not, but Nabopolassar was planning for the far future. He had stored away the stories of how, 200 years ago, our envoys had visited Judah and had been openly shown the glories of the Temple, its treasury, and adjoining palaces by your old King Hezekiah. They had heard old stories of how, following guidance from one of your prophets, he had shut the gates of Jerusalem and defied Sennacherib after that king had destroyed your neighbour Samaria. Was not Isaiah the name of your prophet? The envoys had returned amazed at the wealth they found in Judah, and astonished at the naivety and vanity displayed by Hezekiah in showing it to them. Never forget that these things are noted down and then recounted to future generations. Thus Jerusalem held a special place in his mind. I was flattered that he assigned me to your city as my first posting. I proved adept and gathered information from many sources around the quarters of Jerusalem."

There was an embarrassed shuffling round the room. Suddenly Nebuzaradan switched from Aramaic to Hebrew, taking his audience by surprise, except for Baruch, who appeared amused.

"It was during this posting in Jerusalem that I learned to speak Hebrew, as you hear now. Your fathers were unaware of what was happening, because we made sure that they did not know. We would hardly have been a secret intelligence service if they had! Please be patient. Later I will tell you more."

Boaz burst out "But, my Lord, what do you mean by a bird listening in every palace chamber?"

"I meant it figuratively boy," said Nebuzaradan, in a kindly tone. "It went like this, but I warn you that the details are not savoury," switching back to Aramaic. "Trading on human weakness is never pretty. Clearly we could not insinuate a Babylonian disguised with a false beard into every palace in Nineveh, Assur or elsewhere, to listen behind the curtains. So how does one recruit a local agent? The short answer is first by bribery and then by blackmail. First we identified a set of our merchants who travelled regularly to a city, who were well known there, and could move around without question. We made them our own by paying them much gold and then making sure they remained loyal. Then we taught each one how to identify any avaricious merchant in the target city who might appear open to bribery, in exchange for information: who had serious financial problems; who had a shameful secret to hide; and who was involved in criminal activity to the detriment of his master. Then we would widen the net to members of the palace. The weaknesses and passions of the local governor and those in his bodyguard, army and harem would clearly have been of interest. There are those who would slit your throat if you even glanced at the curtains hiding their womenfolk, however much they may lay hidden, but they cared little for money and let themselves be defrauded at will, while others had a passion for gold and nothing else. Would you be surprised in any empire how much venality is practiced daily on a monumental scale? One never needed to look hard for a victim. Servants and particularly slaves were also good targets for they held a natural resentment against their masters and often gained pleasure from a secret revenge."

"Once approached, many agreed with alacrity, but if they resisted, their pitiful cries of 'I will never betray my beloved people' were quickly silenced by a reminder of what their governor or general would do to them once they had been appraised of certain facts. Then they became very cooperative when they realized that they were actually going to be paid handsomely for nothing more than telling us what they had heard people saying. What was in a few words, a few opinions? Once in receipt of our money they were ours. For them, they had reached the point of no return."

"Multiply this many times over and we had a full picture of the internal state of the government of a city: those on the up and on the down; its financial and military strengths and weaknesses; how hard or flabby it might be when challenged; or the state of health of its leaders and generals and their petty rivalries. Each city was assigned a chief agent who had a budget, pulled the local strings, collated the information and then reported back to us in Babylon using the merchant trains as couriers. These networks took years to build, but once in place they gave us a very full picture of the internal state of the Assyrian Empire. When Ashurbanipal died it was decided that the time had come to break away, particularly since we knew from inside information that the Medes would support us. Even then the Assyrians did not go down without a terrible fight. It was a close run thing and cost us a lot of men. I shudder at memories of the final defeat of Nineveh."[9]

There was a brief silence while he recovered himself with a sip of wine and collected his thoughts.

"My initial task was, as I said, to act as chief agent for Jerusalem, which was how I learned Hebrew. I turned out to be good at this task and was later promoted to be head of this intelligence service, but it

9   612 BCE.

was during this early period when I learned about the discovery of The Book of the Law. One hardly needed to pay an agent to learn of that discovery, for it was public knowledge. It was Hilkiah the High Priest, who made the discovery during the Temple restoration, I recall?"

The men in the room wore an appalled look on their faces. He knew so much. He had known everything from the beginning. Their fathers had been so naive, so open to an enemy, and turned inside out so easily. Many of them hung their heads in shame.

"You were not the only ones, you know," said Nebuzaradan kindly. "We had the same inside knowledge of Egypt, Syria, Moab, Ammon, Edom, Ashkelon, Tyre and everywhere else."

"Now we come to the fourth character in this play of ours. Your King Josiah was an interesting and unusual man. He was still very young but he was just a bit older than us. He seemed so earnest, so open in his attitudes, almost to the point of naivety. You could see it on his face even in public, so unlike your typically cunning monarch who hides everything, even from his own circle. No, not Josiah. When his secretary Shaphan read the Book to him he went crazy with grief, and the shock-waves went round the city. In our Babylonian world, where Marduk is supposed to reign supreme over all the gods, it would be unthinkable to publicly call on a lowly woman like Hulda the Prophetess to ask an opinion, but that was Josiah. I recall that she was the wife of Shallum and lived in the Second Quarter? We knew about her predictions – everyone knew. At the time we did not take any of it seriously. As an old man, I now understand."

"You have to remember that I was young and raised in the Babylonian tradition with her absurd temples, idolatrous ways and superstitious magicians. I knew nothing, or should I say that I was just beginning to learn about Hebrew history, the Law of Moses, the kings of Judah and the Temple tradition, which was so different and so austere. Who had ever heard of a single god controlling our world whom one cannot see but who requires an austere devotion? But what really struck me as odd, very odd, was how much of this had already been rejected, forgotten or dismissed as fantasy by the Judahites themselves. Your Temple had previously been shut for years, to all intents and purposes, and was badly in need of restoration. The son of Hezekiah, Manasseh, had been the bloodiest tyrant in your history, killing some of your old prophets, like Isaiah, in gruesome ways. I heard that he had recanted in the end and had humbled himself but the damage had been done and it could not be undone. He had attempted to destroy the whole heritage of Judah in a fury of bloodletting. There were some, I grant you, who held to the old ways, like Hilkiah and his circle of priests, but most of the populace had become as wild as any Babylonian with an attachment to the most outlandish of shrines. Manasseh had unleashed the whirlwind. There were rumours of even darker deeds of human sacrifice on the hilltop treegroves. Yet Josiah was clearly genuine in his grief and rage over his country and the state of degradation it had reached. Most kings care for little more than the state of their army, treasury, harem and wine cellar. That is what made him different."

"You know, in Babylonian culture the Hebrew idea of repentance has little value. Whatever we feel about what we have done in the past is largely irrelevant. Sexual morality has no meaning. Who cares what men and women do to each other. Maybe the gods care or maybe not. What we fear most is their malevolence by inflicting terrifying dreams that presage bad luck, drought or bad harvests. For this reason they must be appeased. I first learned about the idea of repentance from Josiah who called for both personal and national repentance by urging a radical change of behaviour and attitude. He himself was wholly genuine and took seriously his role as the representative of his nation before the God of Israel. It was quite a spectacle to summon the elders, priests, prophets, and the people to the Temple and read them the Book of the Covenant. I was there, you know. It was quite a thing, I can tell you."

"The main change was in the Temple. The horses and chariots were removed as were the other idols placed there by Manasseh. Then it was cleansed and restored to its old use. Outwardly the people were pleased – they had their special house back – but their pleasure was based on superstitious beliefs. We Babylonians know all about that. You had become one of us, driven by dreams, omens and superstitions.

It was clear to me as an outside observer that his reforms had worked only on a superficial level. People gossiped about them in the squares, and the priests made a big thing of them, but their ingrained daily habits never changed. They had not bitten deep enough, and within a very few short years they were over-turned and we now know the long term consequences."

"Years later, when Josiah rode out to challenge Pharaoh Necho at Megiddo and lost his life in the defeat, I had already been moved to another post, but I am getting ahead of myself. All I can say is that to this day I have never understood why he did it."

"This brings me to Jeremiah the son of Hilkiah. I do recall his first stumbling words: his rebuke to the whole establishment, their astonishment at his effrontery and his nervousness. But then I ought to turn the whole story over to you Baruch?"

Jozadak roused himself to speak. "We are astonished at all this, my Lord. We had no idea. But before Baruch speaks, can you tell us how you and he came to know each other?"

Baruch himself spoke. "Yes, perhaps it makes sense to tell you what lies on the penultimate page of the story. Did you know that after the destruction of the Temple and the walls, my Lord Nebuzaradan here appointed a governor called Gedaliah to govern the small remnant left behind? After the murder of the governor, this remnant of Judahites escaped to Egypt. They took Jeremiah and me with them, much against our will, I might add. In reality, we were their captives. Jeremiah warned them of the consequences but they would not listen."

"We lived in Egypt for a few years among our idolatrous communities that had sprung up there. Jeremiah died of grief and exhaustion some years after. When King Nebuchadnezzar invaded and crushed the Egyptian army, we tried to flee and then hide but the Babylonian army moved so quickly that there was no escape. They were looking for those who had murdered Gedaliah and escaped from Judah. They moved fast. I had been corralled in a compound with the others waiting for the end to come, for we were certain that this time there would be no escape. I recognized my Lord Nebuzaradan here and called out to him in one last desperate bid. How we had been previously acquainted is for another story."

"Oddly, one of my stranger gifts is to remember voices more than faces," said Nebuzaradan. "By then I already knew Jeremiah was dead but I was looking out for Baruch. When he called out I knew it was him immediately. I ordered my men to deal with him kindly and bring him with us. I have had him hidden among you ever since. Rumour was almost correct. Of that group, nobody survived, except Baruch."

4

JEREMIAH: A RELUCTANT YOUNG PROPHET TO THE NATIONS

Baruch spoke gently in an almost wistful, reminiscent tone. "We were boys together of the same age, as were our fathers in Anathoth, a Levitical town. It was only a short walk from Jerusalem of which my grandfather Maaseiah had once been Governor.[10] Every day we were at school together and in and out of each other's houses. Life was different and softer then. We had no idea, no conception, of the cataclysm that was to sweep across us and destroy our world to its roots. Now, each night in my sleep, I remember the names of the dead, for everyone I will speak of, except for my Lord Nebuzaradan here, has been long gone." Tears began to well into his eyes as he recalled his boyhood memories. Boaz watched, amazed, as this remarkable old man, who at times seemed so withdrawn, austere and amused at the world around him, slowly took a long drink of water and recomposed himself. "Ah yes, water is always good for the soul," he declared. "I am ready again now."

---

10   Jer. 32:12 and 2 Chron. 34:8.

The rest of the company in the room waited patiently for him to begin again. His voice gathered strength as he continued.

"Jeremiah was always a sensitive boy, highly-strung, and not given to the rough and tumble of others. His father Hilkiah[11] was a contemporary of Hilkiah, the High Priest who found the Book of the Covenant during the renovation of the Temple in King Josiah's time."

"It began in our middle teens over a period of weeks when he suddenly became nervous and withdrawn in manner, as if something was upsetting him. Then one day, outside the Temple, he appeared on the steps down from the portico while the elders were talking in a group after a meeting. He stepped forward, addressing them and said 'Thus says the LORD.'[12] Everyone was stunned. His voice was shaking as he was trying to overcome extreme nerves. Then he launched off into a speech, clearly meant not just for the elders but also for the public. It was unforgettable. The drama of some events defies description."

Then Baruch began to quote the prophecy of Jeremiah from memory in Hebrew, his accent and cadences from a different age.

"I remember the devotion of your youth, your love as a bride,
how you followed me in the wilderness, in a land not sown.
Israel was holy to the LORD, the first fruits of his harvest.
All who ate of it incurred guilt; disaster came upon them,"
declares the LORD. Hear the word of the LORD, O house of Jacob,
and all the clans of the house of Israel. (Jer. 2:1-3)

"Next came the most devastating indictment. Everyone was trans-fixed, frozen in time, like statues. It was so wholly unexpected."

What wrong did your fathers find in me that they went far

---

11   Was Hilkiah, the father of Jeremiah, the same as Hilkiah the High Priest? It is possible but opinion is divided over this issue.

12   The Tetragrammaton *Yod, He, Waw, He* (written as YHWH in Latin script) is the four-letter biblical name of the God of Israel, without consonants, which the scribes considered too sacred to pronounce. Usually 'ADONAI' (my Lord) was used as a substitute. Christian translations of the Bible into English commonly use LORD in place of the Tetragrammaton. 'Jehovah' came from fusing the vowels of this with the Tetragrammaton.

from me and went after worthlessness, and became worthless?
They did not say, 'Where is the LORD who brought us up from
the land of Egypt, who led us in the wilderness, in a land of
    deserts and pits,
in a land of drought and deep darkness,
in a land that none passes through, where no man dwells?'
And I brought you into a plentiful land to enjoy its fruit
and its good things. But when you came in, you defiled my land
and made my heritage an abomination.
The priests did not say, 'Where is the LORD?'
Those who handle the law did not know me;
the shepherds transgressed against me;
the prophets prophesied by Baal
and went after things that do not profit. (Jer. 2:5-8)

"You look surprised at my quoting? You forget that I was trained as a scribe just like you. Maybe you find my Hebrew accent comically old-fashioned?" he asked with mock severity. "That was how we Levites used to speak in the old days. Also remember that I wrote this. It was under his dictation, but I wrote it. It is forever etched in my memory. Let me continue the story."

"It was as if a thunderclap had fallen across the Temple steps. I will never forget their faces as I have never forgotten the words, as you can see. The mouths of the priests opened and closed like sound-less fish. He was the son of an influential priest who, in turn, was a member of the circle around the High Priest, so they did not openly deride him, but you could see the simultaneous shock and contempt on their faces. The sneers began in private. 'Who *does* he think he is? An impostor! The son of Hilkiah has gone off his head'. It was clear that the speech was a reference to the murderous time of King Manasseh, a generation before, when the prophets and priests of the LORD were tortured and murdered. The accusation against his listeners was based around their acceptance of that new, violent world, its obscene values, including sacrifice to idols and the pagan rituals of calling on demonic spirits. In effect, these had become accepted practices and Jeremiah was accusing his hearers of complicity in their furtherance. The hostile reaction to his words was the product of guilty consciences at work."

"I spoke to him directly afterwards. He was silent, incommunicative, sullen, even. He clearly did not want to talk and shut himself away. After a few days he eased off and began to talk, at least to me. I was puzzled and asked him plainly.

"You were speaking in the first person. You said 'Thus says the LORD'. Did you really mean that?" 'Yes' was his reply to that question – nothing more."

"The Hebrew prophets were also part of our tradition: Samuel and Nathan had both been associated with King David; Amos and Hosea had both denounced Samaria in coruscating fashion; Jonah had his tangle with Nineveh; and then of course, there was the great Isaiah of two centuries ago. Since the hill-top idol-shrines had been functioning, each had had its own 'prophet' or witch-doctor who tried to control his villagers through fear and intimidation. It was a copy and a corruption of the old idol-worship that had sprung up again since Manasseh's reign. Then, in addition to all this, we had our own false prophets of the LORD who skilfully skipped and slid between the political factions making grand declarations of what their masters wanted to hear."

"You see, when you are raised as children together, when you have eaten and been schooled together, you can see in and out of each other's minds. He was bright enough, and absorbed things easily. Of course, since the discovery of the Book, those of us in the circle of families around the High Priest had a renewed interest in the Law. We had studied the content of the writings of the prophets and their poetic styles but Jeremiah himself had never showed any tendency to be a prophetic witness, nor a natural poet. I can certainly vouch for that. Until that moment he had never had a special way with words but when he spoke in public, they just flowed out of him with a surging power. If these prophecies had been his own invention there would have been multiple versions, and close and repeated editing of words and phrases, but there was none. It all came in real time. That was why I was so surprised. He could not possibly have invented words of such penetration and depth himself.[13] Then finally he opened up to me about what had happened."

> Now the word of the LORD came to me, saying,
> "Before I formed you in the womb I knew you,
> and before you were born I consecrated you;
> I appointed you a prophet to the nations."
> Then I said, "Ah, Lord GOD! Behold, I do not know how to speak,
> for I am only a youth."
> But the LORD said to me, "Do not say, 'I am only a youth';
> for to all to whom I send you, you shall go,
> and whatever I command you, you shall speak.
> Do not be afraid of them, for I am with you to deliver you."
> (Jer. 1:4-8)

"He was very reluctant to do this but there was no way out for him."

> Then the LORD put out his hand and touched my mouth and
>   said to me,
> "Behold, I have put my words in your mouth.
> See, I have set you this day over nations and over kingdoms,
> to pluck up and to break down, to destroy
> and to overthrow, to build and to plant." (Jer. 1:9-10)

"Of course, people said 'He's making it up', as they always do, but his words were not vague, ambiguous, grand spiritual allusions with little content. They were pointedly directed at the condition of the populace and the priesthood. In its most practical form the Law of Moses had protected the poor and the weak by allowing them to glean at harvest times but this protection had long ago been ignored. Even children were forced into slavery and denied redress at the courts. Judah had become a brutal, idol-worshiping, blood-sodden, sexually-charged society which flouted the Law without shame. His words hit home hard, even more so because they were true. His reaction, the

---

13   The call of Jeremiah came in 626 BCE.

emotional upset that was plain to see over his features, told the same story. He really did *not* want to do it, for he could see what he was up against, but he felt he had no choice. Jeremiah explicitly asked me to be his secretary and write down what he said in his speeches delivered in the Temple entrance or on the portico."

"Looking back, our world changed forever at that first prophecy on the steps. There was no going back: he was committed and so was I. Despite the sinful ways of Judah, heavily magnified during the reign of Manasseh, and pondered over during that of Josiah, there had been a strange innocence about the attitude of the people, as if they were only half serious in their sinful ways and they could snap out of them at will, or so they thought. It was like the man who drinks too much wine but when chided for it, claims that he can stop any time he likes. That deluded innocence ended right there. Jeremiah's prophecies, so unexpected and genuine in tone, cut right to the bone. It was the real thing – a watershed moment in our history. The time to repent was upon them. Would they turn or not? Despite his reluctance and nervousness, he pressed the point home relentlessly in his public Temple preaching even though I could see it hurt him to do so."

> Run to and fro through the streets of Jerusalem,
> look and take note!
> Search her squares to see if you can find a man,
> one who does justice and seeks truth, that I may pardon her.
> Though they say, 'As the LORD lives,' yet they swear falsely.
> (Jer. 5:1-2)

"He was deeply saddened because at first he had hoped that these words would make his listeners stop and think and then make an attempt to reform their lives. It was if they hesitated for a while but then the general attitude of the populace turned from initial amusement to contemptuous dismissal. Often, outright invective was thrown in his direction. Their refusal to listen and repent hit him very hard."

> O LORD, do not your eyes look for truth?
> You have struck them down, but they felt no anguish;

you have consumed them, but they refused to take correction.
They have made their faces harder than rock;
they have refused to repent. (Jer. 5:3)

"Words are strange and powerful things. They can inspire joy, pride, or even ecstasy, or they can provoke violence. Words can promise and lie simultaneously but the world of words where their meaning has undergone subtle, negotiable changes is particularly dangerous. Once words such as truth, justice and righteousness are placed on a sliding scale then they cease to have any real meaning. The speaker can utter them as smooth platitudes, appearing to conform to certain norms such as the Law of Moses, but then use them as a cover to deny the very things they have apparently promised. When Jeremiah preached, his words were like a waterfall that cut and shredded his hearers.

> "Let the prophet who has a dream tell the dream, but let him who has my word speak my word faithfully. What has straw in common with wheat?" declares the LORD. "Is not my word like fire and like a hammer that breaks the rock in pieces? Therefore, behold, I am against the prophets, who steal my words from one another." (Jer. 23:28-30)

"That is why people reacted so furiously. They were provoked by his words because they were true. They were being publicly shamed about their own sinful behaviour so they lashed out in retaliation. He pleaded with the LORD, asking 'Why me? Why must I carry the burden of this message if they will not listen?' There are times when our God is a hard taskmaster and his calling is irrevocable."

"Those to whom he spoke often used traditional religious language and had all the outward forms yet they behaved in idolatrous ways, indulging in a lurid sexual freedom and a level of violence and brutality that would shock even the people here in Babylon. There were even some who indulged in forms of pagan sacrifice that would freeze your blood if I were to describe them here."

"He then thought that if he spoke to the aristocracy of Judah he might get a response and then work outward from there. He thought that maybe it was only the uneducated poor, who did not know the way of the LORD, the justice of their God? Maybe if he went to the great and spoke to them, they might turn and bring others with them? He was quickly and sadly disabused. They were all the same, having broken the yoke and burst the bonds that had tied them to the LORD. In fact it was even worse because this aristocratic circle spoke so contemptuously of the LORD. They said 'He will do nothing; no disaster will come upon us, nor shall we see sword or famine. The prophets will become wind; the word is not in them' was their response."[14]

"It was after some months of this that he became terribly depressed at the lack of any positive response and withdrew to devote himself to prayer. Then one day, again in public, he came out with these alarming words."

> Behold, I am bringing against you a nation from afar,
> O house of Israel, declares the LORD.
> It is an enduring nation; it is an ancient nation,
> a nation whose language you do not know,
> nor can you understand what they say.
> Their quiver is like an open tomb; they are all mighty warriors.
> They shall eat up your harvest and your food;
> they shall eat up your sons and your daughters;
> they shall eat up your flocks and your herds;
> they shall eat up your vines and your fig trees;
> your fortified cities in which you trust they shall
> beat down with the sword. (Jer. 5:15-17)

"This was the first hint that had been given of invasion and destruction by a foreign power. We now know the result but then, in those early days, it was unthinkable. The general attitude was that Judah was safe because she had the Temple and was under the protection

---

14   Jer. 5:12-13.

of the LORD, however much they despised his word. He challenged them directly."

> An appalling and horrible thing has happened in the land:
> the prophets prophesy falsely, and the priests rule at
> their direction; my people love to have it so,
> but what will you do when the end comes? (Jer. 5:30-31)

Nebuzaradan broke in here in an animated fashion: "That was the point. Few Judahites had travelled widely. They had little conception of the world beyond their own small land on the western edge by the sea. They had just about heard of Lebanon in the north, Moab and Ammon to the east and Syria to the north east for their merchants had been there. The Greeks and the far distant city of Tartessus[15] beyond the sea were just names. They knew nothing of them and cared even less. Egypt was always the traditionally big power. Despite the Assyrian invasion of the previous century, they did *not* understand that Judah lay as a tiny vulnerable country on the western edge of a huge empire. That empire seemed stable at the time so they took this to be the norm, but it never occurred to them that things could change. We Babylonians were about to appear on the horizon and turn the world upside down. Even we had no real conception of the type of rule that Nebuchadnezzar would bring, nor could we have conceived of his murderous, insane rage when defied. Your fathers lived in the moment and thought that their small world would never change, nor would their actions have any consequences. It was a form of sad, deluded ignorance."

Baruch took up his story again. "It had never occurred to them that the survival of little Judah over the centuries, since Joshua through David and to their day, might have had some spiritual significance, especially after the miraculous escape from the Assyrians in the time of Hezekiah. They thought they could do what they liked when they liked, with no consequences, and all would be well. They could not see that they had been protected and that this protection

15   Tartessus lay in the region of Andalusia in modern Spain near the mouth of the Guadalquivir River.

was about to be withdrawn just as the wolf-packs were beginning to circle. They went on blindly, sleep-walking into trouble, just as the biggest wolf of all was about to descend on them."

"It was when his father's generation died that the real trouble began, for they had partly protected him from overt violence," continued Baruch. "His critics then had nothing to restrain them and they let rip. In his innocence he had never imagined that they would turn against him so decisively."

> The LORD made it known to me and I knew;
> then you showed me their deeds.
> But I was like a gentle lamb led to the slaughter.
> I did not know it was against me they devised schemes, saying,
> "Let us destroy the tree with its fruit,
> let us cut him off from the land of the living,
> that his name be remembered no more." (Jer. 11:18-19)

"There were even open threats and a genuine conspiracy against his life in our home town of Anathoth, a Levitical city."

> Therefore thus says the LORD concerning the men of Anathoth, who seek your life, and say, "Do not prophesy in the name of the LORD, or you will die by our hand" – therefore thus says the LORD of hosts: "Behold, I will punish them. The young men shall die by the sword, their sons and their daughters shall die by famine, and none of them shall be left. For I will bring disaster upon the men of Anathoth, the year of their punishment." (Jer. 11:21-23)

"Like most conspiracies, the more people that were involved, the leakier it became. They could not help talking about it, even whispering in public, so the news reached our ears and we hid him away. Nevertheless, it shook him to the core. Many had been family friends, the very circle in which he had been raised. It is my belief he had been secretly hoping that his work was done, that he would get some relief, but the LORD had other plans."

> If you return, O Israel, declares the LORD, to me you should return. If you remove your detestable things from my presence, and do not waver, and if you swear 'As the LORD lives' in truth, in justice, and in righteousness, then nations shall bless themselves in him, and in him shall they glory. For thus says the LORD to the men of Judah and Jerusalem: Break up your fallow ground, and sow not among thorns. Circumcise yourselves to the LORD; and remove the foreskin of your hearts, O men of Judah and inhabitants of Jerusalem; lest my wrath go forth like fire, and burn with none to quench it, because of the evil of your deeds." (Jer. 4:1-4)

"The message was relentless even though he knew what the consequences would be for himself. The strongest words were for the priests, his own kind, who lived in a state of denial. Whereas Manasseh had made a full frontal assault on the followers of the LORD, torturing and murdering many, after him it was the syncretism of the priests who looked both ways. They thought they could remain as priests of the LORD but also indulge in oppressive and pagan practices."

> "Woe to the shepherds who destroy and scatter the sheep of my pasture!" declares the LORD. Therefore thus says the LORD, the God of Israel, concerning the shepherds who care for my people: "You have scattered my flock and have driven them away, and you have not attended to them. Behold, I will attend to you for your evil deeds." (Jer. 23:1-2)

"Next came the turn of the prophets."

> My heart is broken within me; all my bones shake;
> I am like a drunken man, like a man overcome by wine,
> because of the LORD and because of his holy words.

For the land is full of adulterers;
because of the curse the land mourns,
and the pastures of the wilderness are dried up.
Their course is evil, and their might is not right.
"Both prophet and priest are ungodly;
even in my house I have found their evil,"
declares the LORD. (Jer. 23:9-11)

"There always have been and always will be false prophets, but ours were a special breed. They dressed their ideas and false predictions in fancy language which told their hearers what they wished to hear. Their clever words befuddled the minds of their followers with strange messages and prophecies purporting to come from dreams and omens. The more successful were surrounded by considerable entourages and had big followings who virtually worshiped their favourite prophet as a god who was doing us mere mortals a favour by walking the earth."

"Jeremiah's direct, powerful, preaching enraged his hearers, particularly the denunciations of Hananiah and Shemaiah as false prophets. Pashhur the priest, the son of Immer, who was chief officer in the house of the LORD, heard Jeremiah prophesying these things. He beat Jeremiah and put him in the stocks that were in the upper Benjamin Gate of the house of the LORD. The next day, when he was released from the stocks, Jeremiah said to him, 'The LORD does not call your name Pashhur, but Terror on Every Side'."

For thus says the LORD: behold, I will make you a terror to yourself and to all your friends. They shall fall by the sword of their enemies while you look on. And I will give all Judah into the hand of the King of Babylon. He shall carry them captive to Babylon, and shall strike them down with the sword. Moreover, I will give all the wealth of the city, all its gains, all its prized
· belongings, and all the treasures of the kings of Judah into the hand of their enemies, who shall plunder them and seize them and carry them to Babylon. And you, Pashhur, and all who dwell in your house, shall go into captivity. To Babylon you shall go,

and there you shall die, and there you shall be buried, you and all your friends, to whom you have prophesied falsely. (Jer. 20:4-6)

"Can you have any conception how much this made him an outcast, all the more for it being true? Despite a faithful minority, who clung to the LORD and his Word, the bulk looked the other way. Despite the reforms of Josiah, as my Lord Nebuzaradan has said, they pretended to be ministers of the LORD but also indulged in every idol-based whim that took their fancy. Much of this was grim, involving explicit sexual practices in the pagan temples. I need not name them. They are so wearisomely familiar here in Babylon."

5

THE TALE OF THE TWO BASKETS OF FIGS

Nebuzaradan was concentrating intensely on Baruch's story as the web of characters slowly but relentlessly expanded. Baruch gathered himself, took another draught of water, and continued his story. Another member of the party asked "What was the political reaction to Jeremiah's prophecies? We cannot imagine that there was none."

"In the political domain there had not initially been a problem," Baruch answered. King Josiah[16] had supported him but then this unusually godly King was himself killed at Megiddo[17] when Pharaoh Necho marched his Egyptian army north to assist the Assyrians in their war against Babylon. Thereafter the political situation changed. There were even dark rumours that Josiah had been assassinated by a pro-Egyptian court faction, but a veil of silence has hidden the truth."

"The Judahites then chose Josiah's fourth son, Jehoahaz, to succeed him but Pharaoh Necho replaced him with his older brother,

---

16   Josiah ascended the throne in 639 BCE and his reformation began in 621 BCE when the Book of the Law was found in the Temple.

17   609 BCE.

Eliakim, and changed his name to Jehoiakim. Necho imprisoned Jehoahaz at Riblah and later took him to Egypt where he died.[18] But then, after this, in the fourth year of the new King Jehoiakim,[19] Necho was defeated by Prince Nebuchadnezzar at Carchemish[20] and thus the political situation changed dramatically again. Judah was forced to pay tribute to Babylon and bend to her wishes. Jeremiah said this concerning the army of Pharaoh Necho, which Nebuchadnezzar king of Babylon had defeated."

> Prepare buckler and shield, and advance for battle!
> Harness the horses; mount, O horsemen!
> Take your stations with your helmets,
> polish your spears, put on your armour!
> Why have I seen it? They are dismayed and have turned backward.
> Their warriors are beaten down and have fled in haste;
> they look not back – terror on every side! (Jer. 46:3-5)

"It appeared that Egypt was knocked out for good, or so it seemed. The problem was that Necho of Egypt was the favourite despot of the dominant court faction in Jerusalem. His defeat was a setback for them, but King Jehoiakim and his court had still not grasped that the political wind had changed for good. For more than a century they had been left alone on the western edge of the Assyrian Empire, not because of their virtue or Assyrian powerlessness, but because they were considered too insignificant. Babylon was the new power and not only had the muscle to impose its will but the willingness to flex it. However, the court still thought of Egypt as the main power, with the Babylonians as fragile upstarts, to be put in their place in good time. How wrong they were. It was this miscalculation that ultimately led to the tragedy of the Great Siege but, at the back of it, was a hardening

18   2 Kgs 23:31-34.

19   609-597 BCE.

20   605 BCE.

of their hearts against any advice to the contrary. Because Jeremiah said 'Do *not* travel down this road' they were determined to go there."

"The problem was that King Jehoiakim was no follower of the LORD. He had no time for Jeremiah and ordered him to stop all this nonsense. At the beginning of his new reign the LORD told Jeremiah this."

Stand in the court of the LORD's house, and speak to all the cities of Judah that come to worship in the house of the LORD all the words that I command you to speak to them; do not hold back a word. It may be they will listen, and every one turn from his evil way, that I may relent of the disaster that I intend to do to them because of their evil deeds. You shall say to them, "Thus says the LORD: If you will not listen to me, to walk in my law that I have set before you, and to listen to the words of my servants the prophets whom I send to you urgently, though you have not listened, then I will make this house like Shiloh, and I will make this city a curse for all the nations of the earth." (Jer. 26:2-6)

"But more than this, much more, were the explicit threats in his prophecies that the people, the priests and the prophets would be cast out to destruction. A century before, the Assyrians had harried and destroyed the Northern Kingdom in Samaria, but the Judahites said "This could never happen to Judah. No, not to us. After all, we have the Temple". When they were told "Amend your ways and your deeds, and I will let you dwell in this place. Do not trust in these deceptive words: 'This is the Temple of the LORD, the Temple of the LORD, the Temple of the LORD'".[21] For them the Temple had become simply a superstitious charm. As I will explain later, no-one, but no-one, could have ever conceived that the LORD would allow his own Temple to be destroyed and his people taken into captivity, as we have. Its very presence had become a superstition to a godless people."

21   Jer. 7:3-4.

"When he had finished speaking all that he had been commanded to speak, the priests and the prophets and all the people laid hold of him, saying:"

> You shall die! Why have you prophesied in the name of the
> LORD, saying, "This house shall be like Shiloh, and this city shall
> be desolate, without inhabitant?"
> (Jer. 26:8-9)

"The people gathered around Jeremiah and myself in the house of the LORD and insisted that he be put to death because he had prophesied against the city. It was a dramatic moment. We thought we were done for. I must say that despite his timidity he defended himself well, even defiantly, repeating his claims to be a prophet. Then events took a turn. Various elders of the land arose and spoke to all the assembled people, saying, "Micah of Moresheth prophesied in the days of Hezekiah king of Judah, and said to all the people of Judah: 'Zion shall be ploughed as a field; Jerusalem shall become a heap of ruins, and the mountain of the house a wooded height'.[22] Did Hezekiah king of Judah and all Judah put him to death? Did he not fear the LORD and entreat the favour of the LORD, and did not the LORD relent of the disaster that he had pronounced against them? But we are about to bring great disaster upon ourselves"."

"That was a close run thing. They actually did stone to death others who had prophesied."

"Then there was the story about the figs." The occupants of the room looked at Baruch blankly.

"At the time, it rather took my fancy, although its implications stretched the imagination. Some years later, Nebuchadnezzar squashed an attempt by the leaders of Judah to side with Egypt by invading Judah and capturing Jerusalem.[23] King Jehoiakim was captured and put in shackles to be deported but immediately died. His

22   Jer. 2:17-19.

23   597 BCE.

son, the eighteen year old Jehoiachin, became the new King and shut the gates of Jerusalem against Nebuchadnezzar. However, after three months he surrendered and was taken into exile, together with the officials, the craftsmen, and the metal workers. These deportees were your fathers, the families of the second exile. Nebuchadnezzar then replaced Jehoiachin with his uncle Zedekiah (Mattaniah), who was a smiling puppet who danced to everyone's tune."

"After this the LORD showed Jeremiah a vision: two baskets of figs were placed before the Temple. One basket had very good figs, like first-ripe figs, but the other basket had very bad figs, so bad that they could not be eaten. And the LORD said to him, "What do you see, Jeremiah?" He replied, "Figs, the good figs very good, and the bad figs very bad, so bad that they cannot be eaten." Then the word of the LORD came to him."

Like these good figs, so I will regard as good the exiles from Judah, whom I have sent away from this place to the land of the Chaldeans.[24] I will set my eyes on them for good, and I will bring them back to this land. I will build them up, and not tear them down; I will plant them, and not pluck them up. I will give them a heart to know that I am the LORD, and they shall be my people and I will be their God, for they shall return to me with their whole heart.

But thus says the LORD: Like the bad figs that are so bad they cannot be eaten, so will I treat Zedekiah the King of Judah, his officials, the remnant of Jerusalem who remain in this land, and those who dwell in the land of Egypt. I will make them a horror to all the kingdoms of the earth, to be a reproach, a byword, a taunt, and a curse in all the places where I shall drive them. And I will send sword, famine, and pestilence upon them, until they shall be utterly destroyed from the land that I gave to them and their fathers. (Jer. 24:5-10)

24   Chaldea was the more general area of Mesopotamia in which the city of Babylon lay.

"When the situation became worse, and people went back to their idolatrous ways, Jeremiah wrote to the Exiles. This really stoked the flames, for the dominant faction at Court wanted to ally with Egypt and break with Babylon. The problem for him was that this letter was deemed to be a political threat to the Kingdom, and therefore judged to be treasonable words against the King. The threats became more explicit."

It was at this point that Itamar the scribe asked "What about this letter? It talks of the seventy years? How did this come about?"

"Yes, the letter was entrusted to Elasah son of Shaphan and Gemariah son of Hilkiah, whom Zedekiah King of Judah sent to King Nebuchadnezzar in Babylon. It came down heavily on the false prophets and diviners."

> Thus says the LORD of hosts, the God of Israel, to all the exiles whom I have sent into exile from Jerusalem to Babylon: Build houses and live in them; plant gardens and eat their produce. Take wives and have sons and daughters; take wives for your sons, and give your daughters in marriage, that they may bear sons and daughters; multiply there, and do not decrease. But seek the welfare of the city where I have sent you into exile, and pray to the LORD on its behalf, for in its welfare you will find your welfare. For thus says the LORD of hosts, the God of Israel: Do not let your prophets and your diviners who are among you deceive you, and do not listen to the dreams that they dream, for it is a lie that they are prophesying to you in my name; I did not send them, declares the LORD. (Jer. 29:4-9)

"But then we come to the seventy years about which you asked."

> When seventy years are completed for Babylon, I will visit you, and I will fulfil to you my promise and bring you back to this place. For I know the plans I have for you, declares the LORD, plans for welfare and not for evil, to give you a future and a hope. Then you will call upon me and come and pray to me,

and I will hear you. You will seek me and find me, when you seek me with all your heart. I will be found by you, declares the LORD, and I will restore your fortunes and gather you from all the nations and all the places where I have driven you, declares the LORD, and I will bring you back to the place from which I sent you into exile. (Jer. 29:10-14)

"The fact that events worked out exactly the way he predicted did not help him at the time. Of course, there were times when he rebelled. He would hide himself away and refuse to come out. He took it hard that he was the one chosen to say these words and then would have to suffer the consequences. He once said to me. "I am full of the wrath of the LORD; I am weary of holding it in."[25] It was as if he was trying to give up or run away but then it would pour out again from him."

Stand by the roads, and look, and ask for the ancient paths, where the good way is; and walk in it, and find rest for your souls. But they said, "We will not walk in it." (Jer. 6:16)

"He was the messenger whose listeners had become deaf to his words. In the end they walked straight into disaster."

Baruch continued "If his words did not spare Judah, neither did they spare the surrounding nations. He dictated to me a string of prophecies against Moab, Ammon, Edom, Philistia, Egypt, Babylon, Damascus, Kedar and Hazor, just to name some.[26] There were some cryptic pieces of good news among the predictions of disaster. For instance, at the end of the denunciation of Egypt is a passage that goes thus:"

But fear not, O Jacob my servant, nor be dismayed, O Israel, for behold, I will save you from far away, and your offspring from the land of their captivity. Jacob shall return and have quiet and

---

25   Jer. 6:11.

26   These are listed in Jeremiah chapters 46-49.

ease, and none shall make him afraid. Fear not, O Jacob my servant, declares the LORD, for I am with you. I will make a full end
of all the nations to which I have driven you, but of you I will not
make a full end. I will discipline you in just measure, and I will
by no means leave you unpunished. (Jer. 46:27-28)

"All of them came under the lash. Babylon herself will, in time, drink
the cup of the LORD's wrath. Do not doubt it. If he did not spare his
own people, will he spare this evil city?"

Declare among the nations and proclaim, set up a banner and
proclaim, conceal it not, and say: "Babylon is taken, Bel is put to
shame, Marduk is dismayed. Her images are put to shame, her
idols are dismayed." (Jer. 50:2)

Nebuzaradan stirred in his chair. "I have your complete set of scrolls
with me. I have read them. You are right. He will not spare it. Our turn
will come."

Finally Baruch raised his head to the people in the room. "In the
text there was one more word." Everyone looked at him, expecting
to hear the name of another country or city. "It was about me," he
said quietly.

Thus says the LORD, the God of Israel, to you, O Baruch: You
said, "Woe is me! For the LORD has added sorrow to my pain. I
am weary with my groaning, and I find no rest." Thus shall you
say to him, Thus says the LORD: Behold, what I have built I am
breaking down, and what I have planted I am plucking up – that
is, the whole land. And do you seek great things for yourself?
Seek them not, for behold, I am bringing disaster upon all flesh,
declares the LORD. But I will give you your life as a prize of war
in all places to which you may go. (Jer. 45:2-5)

"At the time I had no idea what this meant. In my younger days I had
hopes of great things, but which young man does not? At one time,

my grandfather was governor of Jerusalem. I also had hopes during the reformation of Josiah that things would go well and the kingdom would turn back to the LORD. Any hopes of advancement had disappeared as my association with Jeremiah became stronger. We were both outcasts and both of us took this hard, but we were very different personalities. I was more aggressive in my youth, an arguer and a fighter, whereas he was much more sensitive. I had no idea at the time how much of an outcast I was to become. The fact that I am speaking to you here tonight is a fulfilment of that prophecy, as you can see. Like Jeremiah, I never had a family. He was my only friend and he has been dead these many years. The way of the LORD with the children of men can be a hard and difficult road."

DANIEL AND NEBUCHADNEZZAR

"Nebuchadnezzar grew into the strangest man I have ever known, and I have met un-countably many in my 90 years." As he spoke, Nebuzaradan's old, lined face clouded as he reminisced over matters from his youth. "In contrast, Daniel was the most remarkable man I have ever met in terms of ability, calmness and trusting faith in the God of Israel. The two together were perhaps the oddest, contrasting pair in history, yet their lives were inextricably linked. I cannot tell the story of one without the other."

"In his best years, old King Nabopolassar, Nebuchadnezzar's father, was a realist. He planned every move well ahead of time, down to the last detail. Nothing was left to chance. He was born into modest wealth and rose to become an Assyrian governor relatively young, but he understood the realities of power and its limits, for he had experienced the vicissitudes of the Assyrian royal court. Moreover, there is a big difference between comfortable wealth that enables you to live well, and the insatiable desire for unlimited wealth that is akin to a creeping disease: mountains of gold, heaps of flashing jewels beyond counting and lands and vineyards that cover the earth. He never suffered from this malady, but in his later years he was unable to control our princes, many of them his younger sons, who suffered from this illness and whose greed grew to monstrous proportions. It is always the same: the young are impatient to take the reins of power and make the mistakes their over-cautious elders are anxious to avoid. Members of the circle around Crown Prince Nebuchadnezzar were like vicious hungry wolves who leave nothing for the morning. They wanted it all and they wanted it immediately."

"Nebuchadnezzar himself had immense ability and authority. He grew up with it and it came naturally to him but now, looking back, even in his youth there was a certain strangeness about him with an odd luminosity in his eyes when he spoke to you as if he was observing you from a different world through a screen. You could not work out what was going on in his head as if he was not mentally sitting there in the same room. In his youth he had been forced by circumstance to concentrate on Babylon's military campaigns and it was probably the ferocity of those that kept him in check. There is nothing like having the command of men in wartime to discipline a man. The results on the battlefield cannot be hidden, so if you are neglectful and wasteful of lives, an incompetent strategist and a poor planner, you will always be exposed and your allies and mercenaries will desert you. In reality Nebuchadnezzar was a good general, always on the front foot. He forced his enemies into mistakes and then exploited these to the full. It was only after he became King that the cracks began to show, beginning with wild threats against his servants or peculiar cruelties he would dream up for those who failed to satisfy his whims. They were the first sign that something was not right in his head."

"You would have already known that Daniel came here from Jerusalem with a batch of teenage boys whom we demanded from every country who paid tribute to us. In effect, they were your first set of deportees although, at the time, it seemed merely like a token goodwill gesture.[27] No-one could have predicted how it was going to turn out. For all the realism of his youth and middle age, in his older years Nabopolassar developed an idealistic streak. He said "If we take

---

27   About 606 BCE.

these boys and train them in our language and ways, we can send them home and then they can teach their own people our culture and methods. Then they will become our friends and not our enemies." Perhaps he was losing his grip. Too much wine does this to old men."

He made a wry face at Boaz and smiled. "He never grasped the point that people want to govern themselves. The natural order of things suggests that they prefer a stupid king of their own people to a gifted foreigner who will always be a tyrant in their eyes. Nabopolassar had been too sharp at his best to fully realize the average level of human cussedness. Moreover, he never grasped the unique history of Judah and the place your God held in its history."

"Nebuchadnezzar was campaigning in the west against the Egyptians and Assyrians just after your King Josiah was killed at Megiddo. It came to a head at the battle of Carchemish in the bend in the Euphrates.[28] I was there. We defeated the Egyptians with ease – they were no match for us. We found that their mercenaries were useless and just melted away.[29] We knew all their positions and dispositions in advance, as I explained earlier, whereas they had no idea what they were up against. Just weeks after that, the news came through that Nabopolassar had died. Nebuchadnezzar took his royal guard, of which I was one, and rode over the desert at speed to reach Babylon fast – that was some ride. No-one, but no-one, was going to usurp his throne after all the years he had waited for the prize. Nebuchadnezzar and the princes in his circle were ecstatic and could not hide their glee. It was a new age for new men and they were determined to enjoy the fruits. The ultimate problem lay in the cost that others had to pay."

"You know how we Babylonians are obsessed with dreams and omens. How people think the gods are speaking to them by looking at the entrails of a bird I shall never know, but there it is. With some it becomes an obsession. The enchanters and sorcerers make a fat living by predicting nonsense, swooping around in robes adorned with ridiculous symbols. Of course, by accident, they occasionally get

28   605 BCE.

29   Jer. 46:21.

things right. People remember only those occasions and none of the much greater number when they were wrong. Daniel and his friends were trained in these ways, as were all our imports. Despite the fact that they were forced to go through a training in all our Babylonian nonsense they never gave up or forgot their rigorous training in the Hebrew Scriptures, although that had to be a covert thing."

"Most of you are scribes, so you already know that we Babylonians think of Nebo as a scribe to the gods who have the power to shorten or prolong life. Indeed, Nebuchadnezzar's name means "Nebo has established the boundary," thus expressing faith in Nebo. You also know that the dream-world is important to us because it is thought to be the dwelling place of the spirits of men who had experienced unhappy lives or who had suffered violent death. These ghosts are sent to torment the living through the dreams we all experience."

"One night Nebuchadnezzar had a vivid dream. It frightened him to such a degree that he got the shakes but then, like most dreams, he could not remember what it was. His over-developed sense of the dramatic was well-known to his courtiers but in this case the effect was real – he was shaking uncontrollably. He called on the dream merchants around the court – these people even had special titles – to tell him what it was. He could neither remember nor explain the dream but he was badly frightened by it. They could neither tell him the dream nor its meaning, which drove him into a monstrous rage, a sort of manic fury which we had never seen before. He declared their lives forfeit if they could not tell him the dream and its interpretation. Daniel was part of their stable. Everyone was in a spin. We all thought that was it: executions galore and time for others to move in and pick up the spoils. The imported boys would just be collateral damage in the carnage."

"But then your boy Daniel stepped forward. He and his three friends were different. Rumour had it, which he confirmed to me later, that they had secretly been allowed to eat their own food, a frugal vegetable diet by our standards. They had put their case to their keeper Ashpenaz over their desire to stick to a diet that conformed to the laws of Moses. At first Ashpenaz was reluctant but he agreed to a trial. In a few weeks they looked lean and sinuous and much fitter than the others. After that he was always willing to listen to them. Ashpanez went to my predecessor Arioch, Captain of the Royal Guard, and told him that his boy Daniel could interpret the King's dream. Apparently Daniel and his three friends had been praying all night. The rumour spread like wildfire round the court. This news was like honey to Arioch who was secretly alarmed at having to carry out the sentence. He grasped at this seeming off-chance and immediately brought Daniel before the King."

"Others would have been shaking in their sandals but Daniel was as calm and cool as a mild breeze on a day in summer."

From the folds of his cloak in the chair Nebuzaradan took out a scroll. "My eyes are not what they were. Boaz, can you read the Aramaic for me from this scroll that Daniel wrote? Good – here and here," indicating the parts in the scroll. The boy read out the text fluently to the room.

> You saw, O King, and behold, a great image. This image, mighty and of exceeding brightness, stood before you, and its appearance was frightening. The head of this image was of fine gold, its chest and arms of silver, its middle and thighs of bronze, its legs of iron, its feet partly of iron and partly of clay. As you looked, a stone was cut out by no human hand, and it struck the image on its feet of iron and clay, and broke them in pieces. Then the iron, the clay, the bronze, the silver, and the gold, all together were broken in pieces, and became like the chaff of the summer threshing floors; and the wind carried them away, so that not a trace of them could be found. But the stone that struck the image became a great mountain and filled the whole earth.

> This was the dream. Now we will tell the king its interpretation. You, O King, the King of Kings, to whom the God of heaven has given the kingdom, the power, and the might, and the glory, and into whose hand he has given, wherever they dwell, the children of man, the beasts of the field, and the birds of the heavens,

· making you rule over them all – you are the head of gold. Another kingdom inferior to you shall arise after you, and yet a third kingdom of bronze, which shall rule over all the earth. And there shall be a fourth kingdom, strong as iron, because iron breaks to pieces and shatters all things. And like iron that crushes, it shall break and crush all these. And as you saw the feet and toes, partly of potter's clay and partly of iron, it shall be a divided kingdom, but some of the firmness of iron shall be in it, just as you saw iron mixed with the soft clay. And as the toes of the feet were partly iron and partly clay, so the kingdom shall be partly strong and partly brittle. As you saw the iron mixed with soft clay, so they will mix with one another in marriage, but they will not hold together, just as iron does not mix with clay. And in the days of those Kings the God of heaven will set up a kingdom that shall never be destroyed, nor shall the kingdom be left to another people. It shall break in pieces all these kingdoms and bring them to an end, and it shall stand forever, just as you saw that a stone was cut from a mountain by no human hand, and that it broke in pieces the iron, the bronze, the clay, the silver, and the gold. A great God has made known to the King what shall be after this. The dream is certain, and its interpretation sure. (Dan. 2:31-45)

The atmosphere in the room was charged like lightning. The faces of Boaz and the other men in the room had a rapt look as if they had been hypnotized.

Nebuzaradan put the scroll down and said "Yes, it is quite a story, is it not? Dazzling statues, stones sent from heaven, nations and kingdoms rising and falling. Not your usual run of the mill nonsense with incantations and the entrails of snakes."

His story continued: "You should have seen Nebuchadnezzar's face! All the rage had drained away leaving his visage glowing with relief and wonderment. His admiration for Daniel was something to behold. He almost fell over himself with gratitude. Moreover, he loved being at the centre of things. To be that "Head of Gold" flattered his vanity. The meaning of the rest of it had passed him by."

"Human nature is strange. An idealist would say "O, surely the Babylonian magicians must have been so grateful to Daniel for saving their lives!" Not one whit. No-one enjoys indebtedness to another and they owed their lives to him. After this, the King put huge swathes of power into Daniel's hands, at which point the other courtiers ground their teeth in silent rage. If our Court excels in anything it is murderous jealousy tinged with hypocrisy and sycophancy. Of course, Daniel was a supremely gifted administrator. That intelligent, cool, calm, temperament of his was perfect to run a series of dull departments whose function actually matters to the efficient running of an empire. Soldiers have to be fed and paid, taxes have to be gathered and the bureaucracy has to be coaxed into working. His problem was his probity. He could not be flattered and he could not be bought, whereas daily corruption on a grand scale was the standard currency of our government. He changed all that and thus several fountains of gold that fed the voracity of the princes were shut off at source. They were furious and wanted rid of him but they could not see how."

"Their poison festered in silence for some time until one day they saw their opportunity. Daniel had three friends called Hananiah, Mishael and Azariah, renamed as Shadrach, Meshach and Abednego in our language. The new name given to Daniel was Belteshazzar. The King refused him nothing, so on his request they were made administrators of the provinces."

"It was the King himself who was the precursor to the next part of the story. The statue with the head of gold appearing in his dream literally went to his head, so he decided to build a statue of gold of height sixty cubits and six cubits wide. All that gold! Then he sent for everyone in his court – everyone – to worship this statue. The signal was that when the music began, everyone was to bow low. That was no problem for us Babylonians – we can do image worship any and every day of the week, as you know – but it was a problem for Shadrach, Meshach and Abednego. They would have quietly ignored it and melted into the background but their court enemies made sure the King knew of their refusal."

"He then went into one of his famous rages. Was he not the Head of Gold? Had not this come from heaven? Was he not the Great King over all the earth? How dare they refuse to obey his orders? He ordered this huge metal oven to be heated by logs and then threatened them with it if they refused to comply. Some whispered 'Why do you not just do it? It means nothing?' but they were adamant. Like Daniel they were as cool as running water and answered the King that they had no need to answer him in this matter.[30] Their God, whom they served, was able to deliver them from the burning fiery furnace, and would deliver them out of his hand. But even if he did not, they would not serve his gods or worship the golden image that he had set up."

"Nebuchadnezzar never could hide his feelings, even less his rage. You should have seen his face! He was like a thwarted child who had had a toy forcibly removed from his grasp. In his mountainous fury he commanded them to be thrown into this furnace. You would have expected a hissing and a smell of burning flesh but there was none. Everyone was puzzled including the King who rushed over to look and declared that he saw them walking in the fire. Moreover, he saw a fourth who had the appearance of a son of the gods! He commanded that Shadrach, Meshach and Abednego come out!"

"So out they walked untouched. We were amazed and for the second time the King was astonished, amazed and alarmed and ended up fawning over them. In the end they had even more power than before and the princes gnashed their teeth until the blood ran."

"The story is not over yet. Nebuchadnezzar had another dream. This time he could remember it. Daniel also recorded it and it went like this:"

> The visions of my head as I lay in bed were these: I saw, and behold, a tree in the midst of the earth, and its height was great. The tree grew and became strong, and its top reached to heaven, and it was visible to the end of the whole earth. Its leaves were

---

30 Dan. 3:16-18.

beautiful and its fruit abundant, and in it was food for all. The beasts of the field found shade under it, and the birds of the heavens lived in its branches, and all flesh was fed from it. I saw in the visions of my head as I lay in bed, and behold, a watcher, a holy one, came down from heaven. He proclaimed aloud and said thus: "Chop down the tree and lop off its branches, strip off its leaves and scatter its fruit. Let the beasts flee from under it and the birds from its branches. But leave the stump of its roots in the earth, bound with a band of iron and bronze, amid the tender grass of the field. Let him be wet with the dew of heaven. Let his portion be with the beasts in the grass of the earth. Let his mind be changed from a man's, and let a beast's mind be given to him; and let seven periods of time pass over him. The sentence is by the decree of the watchers, the decision by the word of the holy ones, to the end that the living may know that the Most High rules the kingdom of men and gives it to whom he will and sets over it the lowliest of men." (Dan. 4:10-17)

"He called in Daniel to interpret it. It was bad news for the King and you could see that he was visibly dismayed at having to deliver it."

It is you, O King, who have grown and become strong. Your greatness has grown and reaches to heaven, and your dominion to the ends of the earth. And because the King saw a watcher, a holy one, coming down from heaven and saying, "Chop down the tree and destroy it, but leave the stump of its roots in the earth, bound with a band of iron and bronze, in the tender grass of the field, and let him be wet with the dew of heaven, and let his portion be with the beasts of the field, till seven periods of time pass over him". This is the interpretation, O King: It is a decree of the Most High, which has come upon my Lord the King, that you shall be driven from among men, and your dwelling shall be with the beasts of the field. You shall be made to eat grass like an ox, and you shall be wet with the dew of heaven, and seven periods of time shall pass over you, till you know that the Most High rules the kingdom of men and gives it to whom he will. And as it was commanded to leave the stump of the roots of the tree, your kingdom shall be confirmed for you from the time that you know that Heaven rules. Therefore, O King, let my counsel be acceptable to you: break off your sins by practicing righteousness, and your iniquities by showing mercy to the oppressed, that there may perhaps be a lengthening of your prosperity. (Dan. 4:22-27)

"The King did not really grasp the main point that this was about his behaviour and attitudes. He had always thought he could do as he wished. Was he not that great Head of Gold in his first dream, the greatest being on earth? His understanding of his first dream stopped at the point of the special place he held in the scheme of things but he failed to see that he nevertheless lay under the authority of the God of Heaven. Instead, he took upon himself the mantle of God. His cruelties and rages grew ever greater, mainly because he could not stand being defied. Even attempts to discuss a question from every angle brought down his ire. Ultimately he went on to commit the greatest sin of all. He finally decided he was the God of Heaven and attributed to himself the creation of the glory of Babylon, its gardens, walls and fountains. He even declared this from the city walls in public. As Judahites, you will understand that this is the ultimate sin. Even we sinful Babylonians shy away from such a claim as this."

"The root cause was the sickness of mind that had been growing from his youth. You recall that I mentioned earlier about the strange streak in his personality? This now came upon him with greater force. It intensified and about a year after his declaration from the city walls he began to grow so sick that he reached the stage where he could no longer recognize people, even his own sons and daughters. Finally he fell into a trance. He was conscious but he began to mutter strange, unintelligible sounds and crawl around outside. Worse, he began to eat grass and not normal food. We had to hide him away under special guard and put it about that the King was indisposed. Over the weeks, strange physical changes in his body occurred. His nails grew thick and rough and his hair long and coarse. To all intents and purposed he had changed into an animal. He lived mainly outside and ate grass and he was otherwise healthy in body but it was clear that in his mind he thought he was an ox or a bull.[31] It was not only wholly remarkable but also wholly alarming and upsetting. What does one do with a mad King who has become an animal, to all intents and purposes? The priests and sorcerers whispered about possession but they had no idea what to do. Their stupid incantations were useless. Moreover, we had no idea what to do either! Then slowly, very slowly, the process went into reverse. He began to lift his head and look around and up at the sky, slowly whispering as he did so. Then he stood upright again, began to eat normal food, and then finally he began to speak again, firstly in a whisper, then in a rational manner. He then issued a decree acknowledging the God of Heaven. He was never entirely the same as before, which was perhaps for the better, but he was the King again. After that he was more humble in mind and spirit. It was if he had finally understood what Daniel had meant in the interpretation of his dream 'until you know that the Most High rules the kingdom of men and gives it to whom he will'."

"As for Daniel, he continued for many years as an administrator, trusted by the King, but distrusted by the princes. In the Guard and the Army we made sure he was not touched. The princes have great power and will do many things but they dare not challenge us. He is in private retirement now, and protected. He spends much time in calm, silent prayer, facing Jerusalem. He has lived a life well spent, in such a way that a man ought to live. I will say this of him that he was, and still is, the most remarkable man I have ever met."

---

31 R. K. Harrison (Introduction to the Old Testament, IVP, 1975) provides cogent arguments that suggest that Nebuchadnezzar was suffering from an exceptionally rare mental disorder called Boanthropy.

7

JUDAH: FROM BRIGHT NEW DAY TO DARKEST NIGHT

Nights in the city were variable. The Great River dragged the tracks of the myriad desert breezes in its swirling wake, deflecting and distorting their paths. Some had the warm, dry, spicy smell of the desert, hinting at the seasonal gritty storms to come. Others carried a heavy, humid river smell of reed beds and rotting vegetation. The worst came from the direction of the vast camps carrying the odours of tens of thousands of unwashed, grief-stricken, labouring bodies, quarry dust and the fires of brick kilns. Those acrid breezes caught in the throat and induced a nasty coppery taste on the tongue. Tonight, none of these breezes stirred the warm, humid, stillness that invited contemplation of the clear night sky.

The elders were out in a courtyard taking a break from the airless room, even though it was open and well-ventilated. Boaz wondered at the source of the heat? Was it from their own flustered and fearful state? Nebuzaradan, a shrewd observer, had wisely suggested a short break. A guard from the troop under the command of the young

officer stood by the wall in a relaxed pose, with the concerned air of a
shepherd looking over his flock. Boaz imagined that his ancestors had
been shepherds but decided not to ask.

In a corner of the courtyard the scribe Itamar came over to stand
still and silent by his side. Despite his teaching gifts, Itamar had never
been one for chatter and had always chosen his words carefully. Boaz
felt easy in his company. His gift of natural silence made the listener
more alert when there was something important to be said. "I think
I can divine your thoughts, Boaz? You are angry, are you not, asking
yourself 'why have we not been told any of this'? Am I correct?"

Boaz was not a naturally rebellious boy so his own reactions
alarmed him. He nodded "Yes, sir, that is exactly what I am thinking.
I *do* feel a rising anger but I cannot understand why."

"Our silence on these matters concerning Jeremiah has never
been due to a policy of deliberate concealment, but we have never
known what it all means, what to say about it, and how to tell your
generation. The story has not yet finished, as you can see. The scrolls
of his earlier prophecies have been in our possession from before the
Great Siege, delivered by Baruch himself I was once told, but none of
us know the end story. I suspect and indeed hope that we will hear this
from him. I am astonished that he is still alive, living here in Babylon
in plain sight. It is indeed a miracle that he has been preserved for so
long. You heard the gasps in the room when Nebuzaradan introduced
him? You must remember that the events recounted here tonight may
seem a long time ago to you, but in terms of the history of our people it
is too close for understanding. For instance, we have the strange written prophecies of Ezekiel, who was one of us Exiles, but we have no idea
what they mean. The fact that we are here tonight means that this story
is not complete but is still unfolding and we are part of it. One day we
may understand its significance in the great scheme of things."

After a short silence, while Boaz tried to still the whirling questions in his mind. Itamar coughed gently in his own prim, slightly
self-effacing way: "In fact I can safely say that I am agog to hear more.
I have often taught you, have I not, that the God of Israel will never

desert his people, even though we are but a remnant? Once we were a slave people in Egypt's land but He rescued us, as our Passover remembers and celebrates. Now we are in exile again, a different Egypt and a different form of slavery, but in exile nevertheless. He will rescue us again. Despite our sins and rebellion, he loves us with an unending love. I know, I know, this all sounds so tediously pious to your young, impatient ears while your mind asks 'But when, where, how?' The truth is, I do not know. You are a young bright scholar, with real ability and a strong questioning mind, which is good, but tonight we have reached the edge of the chasm that lies between intellectual adolescence and adulthood. You are on the edge between learning facts that have already been discovered by others and digging out hard-won truths for yourself."

"I cannot tell you how the God of Israel will rescue us from this captivity but I am convinced that he will. Did our God make the whole world and the stars just for our benefit alone? If he is that big, does he not have a purpose for the whole world? As his children, our task was to *live* as the people of God, to live *righteously*, so that his Great Name would be glorified among the nations of the Earth. Instead, we spent our time in self-indulgence and forgot him. Now, within our remnant, there is a desire to go home and begin again."

He then raised his hand in emphasis. "Sometimes it feels as if he has forgotten us but now, tonight, is such a time when I can sense that his hand is upon us. Idolaters think their little gods rule the rocks, rivers and trees in their localities, but surely the lesson we learn from Daniel's story is that his hand is everywhere, even here in Babylon, at the centre of a corrupt Empire. Stay awake, be alert and listen, for this is not a school lesson. It is clear to me that you have a part to play in the coming events, otherwise why are you here? Why was it that it was *your* questioning that began all this? *Remember, our God does not carry passengers when taking his people on a journey – the sceptical, rebellious generation that fell in the desert is a witness to that.* I am getting old and my time is past. Maybe my journey is about to end, in which case the torch will soon pass on to you, so take some fruit and some well-water with just a hint of this beautiful wine to help you concentrate, because it is going to be a very long night."

It was time to reconvene. The elders were now more composed and ready to listen. Reeling a little from the heavy emphases of his talk with Itamar, who normally jousted in subtle hints and allusions, Boaz' senses were on edge. Nebuzaradan was in a jovial mood. "Most of you were born here so you know that we Babylonians normally drink beer, not wine, but I learned to like it when I was stationed in Jerusalem. I can see, Boaz, that you are trying it in your water? That is the best way if you wish to stay awake."

It was Jozadak, the lofty High Priest, who brought them back to the point to ask sadly, "How did we come to this? Jerusalem, the home of the Temple, is now in ruins and our people in exile. Once we were a sun-drenched, rich, exotic land, a beacon to the nations, or so we thought. We have been brought so low that we are a reproach and darkest night surrounds us. Will this nightmare ever end? Will we ever return?"

Turning to his audience, Baruch said "How did a nation such as ours come to reject our own history? I am aware that you know many of the things I am going to tell you but bear with me for a while and you might learn more. Ours was a glorious history that began with Abraham, the line of which could then be traced through Isaac, Jacob and the twelve Patriarchs, the Exodus, the receiving of the Law of Moses on Sinai, the entry into Canaan after the forty years in the desert and then the Davidic line of kings. Our book of Exodus summarizes our relation with the God of Israel."

You yourselves have seen what I did to the Egyptians, and how I bore you on eagles' wings and brought you to myself. Now therefore, if you will indeed obey my voice and keep my covenant, you shall be my treasured possession among all peoples, for all the

earth is mine; and you shall be to me a kingdom of priests and a
holy nation. (Ex. 19:4-6)

"There is no nation on this earth with a history like ours, so how
did we come to forget? In reality, the normal state of this world is a
place where evil flourishes and kingdoms invade, plunder and enslave
others. Huge numbers die in the misery of slavery, never having
known their parents, with their own children living short, starving,
miserable lives. Many die in agonizing sickness. This has been its true
state since evil entered the world. Life has never been normal since
then. Calamities in this life do not happen as some act of fickle, spon-
taneous, divine retribution, like a hammer coming down randomly
from heaven. People have it the wrong way round. They think of the
good life with peace, security and adequate food as the normal state
of the world, even what is due to them, and when this peace is shat-
tered they cannot understand. 'How could God do this to me?' goes up
the cry when trouble strikes."

"Look around you here in Babylon? You see the remnant of peoples plundered and ravished. Our fathers once knew what slavery was
like in Egypt but we were rescued by the divine hand of him who rules
the earth, who guided us into a safe land where we could grow and
rest. Did Judah and the other tribes of our people really think that the
centuries of peace in their little lands was the norm, due to them by
right? It clearly had not occurred to us that we had been given the Law
of Moses for a reason, as a way to guide our lives, nor had it occurred
to us that we had been divinely protected. We were arrogant enough
to think that we could ignore all the warning signs and wander off to
behave in wilful ways. We assumed that the food, peace and security
were all ours by right. When the wolves began to circle, to whom did
we turn? Hezekiah turned his face to the LORD and was answered at
the great Assyrian Siege almost two centuries ago. In her last years
Judah did not turn back to the ancient paths of her fathers but chose
to continue to worship loathsome idols – the reign of Manasseh was
the watershed. Let go of your anchor and cast off from your roots
and the wind will carry you not only to places of which you never

dreamed, but also to places which were once the stuff of your worst nightmares. Then you discover that there is no way back. We chose to reject our own history from the Patriarchs and Moses onward. We chose to go our own way and were left to our own devices. It was as if our God said to us 'Well, you have consistently ignored me and forged your own way – so be it. Find your own path.' Indeed, people who take this road end up losing their judgment and their minds. Ultimately, we forgot that we were his treasured possession, tripped over ourselves and became the prey of the biggest, sharpest-toothed wolf of all. In a blind panic, what is the use of sacrificing to ghosts and spirits and praying for deliverance to idols made of wood and decorated with gold and silver? Will he rescue us again, as he did from Egypt? Yes, I believe he will, but *how* I do not know."

"The root of the trouble began with Solomon and his wives. In his youth, Solomon was a great man in every sense of the word. He was richly endowed with great spiritual wisdom, well beyond his years. He had immense wealth and he was fortunate enough to live in a time of relative peace so all of these good gifts could be enjoyed. His problem was that in later life he wrecked everything by over-indulgence and allowed wild practices that grew and could not be tamed."

"David of Bethlehem, his father, first appeared as the miraculous young shepherd-boy slayer of the giant Goliath of Gath in one of Saul's great confrontations with the Philistines. After seven years on the throne of Judah, and a further thirty three on the throne of the full twelve tribes of the Kingdom of Israel, David spent his life as a soldier, poet and singer. I believe we all know that he was a very great man who was also a highly flawed individual. After the disastrous rebellion and death of his son Absalom he poured everything he knew into Solomon and saved his nation's wealth and his own so that Solomon would have the resources to build the Temple. The expenditure of gold and bronze, never mind cedar-wood, was astronomical. Solomon may have ultimately built it but it had been planned and financed by David. He had even laid out the rules and regulations for the priests and singers."

"The Temple was a magnificent achievement of engineering and high art combined. No-one had seen anything like it and might never again, at least not in its original form, but it had a significance that went far beyond a grand artistic statement. It contained the Ark of the Covenant, set in the Most Holy Place, which could only be entered once a year by the High Priest on the Day of Atonement. The Ark contained the Tablets of the Law and Aaron's staff that had budded. At the inauguration of the Temple, Solomon said this."

O LORD, God of Israel, there is no God like you, in heaven above or on earth beneath, keeping covenant and showing steadfast love to your servants who walk before you with all their heart; you have kept with your servant David my father what you declared to him. You spoke with your mouth, and with your hand have fulfilled it this day. Now therefore, O LORD, God of Israel, keep for your servant David my father what you have promised him, saying, 'You shall not lack a man to sit before me on the throne of Israel, if only your sons pay close attention to their way, to walk before me as you have walked before me.' Now therefore, O God of Israel, let your word be confirmed, which you have spoken to your servant David my father. (1 Kgs. 8:23-26)

"I think Solomon genuinely understood the issue: the Temple was a symbolic place where God would dwell with his people and would continue to do as long as they remained faithful – it was a conditional promise. There is a very interesting part of this prayer that specifically talks of disobedience and captivity."

If they sin against you – for there is no one who does not sin – and you are angry with them and give them to an enemy, so that they are carried away captive to the land of the enemy, far off or near, yet if they turn their heart in the land to which they have been carried captive, and repent and plead with you in the land of their captors, saying, "We have sinned and have acted perversely and wickedly," if they repent with all their heart and with all their soul in the land of their enemies, who carried them captive, and pray to you toward their land, which you gave to their fathers, the city that you have chosen, and the house that I have built for your name, then hear in heaven your dwelling place their prayer and their plea, and maintain their cause and forgive your people who have sinned against you, and all their transgressions that they have committed against you, and grant them compassion in the sight of those who carried them captive, that they may have compassion on them (for they are your people, and your heritage, which you brought out of Egypt, from the midst of the iron furnace). Let your eyes be open to the plea of your servant and to the plea of your people Israel, giving ear to them whenever they call to you. For you separated them from among all the peoples of the earth to be your heritage, as you declared through Moses your servant, when you brought our fathers out of Egypt, O Lord GOD. (1 Kgs. 8:26-53)

"No one could have expressed things in this manner without having truly understood what he was saying. In his youth and middle age Solomon dazzled everyone. He had a penetrating spiritual and worldly wisdom that belied his years. His proverbs had a depth of wisdom and understanding of the human heart, and a way of expressing those thoughts in words that lay beyond normal penetration. Truly you could say that these gifts were God-given. He also had wealth beyond your wildest dreams, even those of Babylonian princes, particularly with the tribute from the surrounding nations pouring in full flow. People felt that their King knew everything and could see through everything, but his one weakness was women. Women flocked to him and round him, delighting in his wit, wealth and intelligence. Indeed he took full advantage. He ended up with 700 wives and 300 concubines. I have often wondered where on earth he housed them. They must have been scattered all over Israel, for there could never have been room in the palaces of Jerusalem for all of them, each with scores of servants and children. The expenditure must have been mountainous."

"If he had been content with Israelite women alone, it might have resulted in less damage but he insisted on marrying foreign wives from the surrounding nations. I think he convinced himself that it was a subtle form of diplomacy. It was these wives who brought with them and their servants their habits of idol worship from Moab, Ammon, Tyre and other places. It is a lesson in how just one weakness, sown among many great strengths, can lead to trouble."

"And serious trouble it turned out to be. None of you will have learned about the habits of these idol worshippers?" he asked. There was a shaking of heads.

"I suppose not, because the worship of those idols were the sins of our fathers, so they have rightly have been hidden from you. It was through Solomon that they were re-introduced into Israel. Moloch (Milcom) was a Canaanite deity. The idol was comprised of a hollow bronze statue heated by fire from within. Children were sacrificed by burning on his red-hot arms heated from within. Having been driven out of Israel a generation before the worship of Moloch was re-introduced by the Ammonite women. Solomon was also said to have built a sanctuary to Chemosh, the god of the Moabites, on the Mount of Olives.[32] Then there were the endless Canaanite fertility gods. One could argue that his introduction of these were diplomatic gestures to the Kings of the surrounding nations, some of whose daughters he was marrying. It is possible but somehow I doubt it. In old age I think he lost his mind and his judgment and allowed all those beautiful women to cajole and coax him into allowing them their own way. It was not just a national but also a personal tragedy. This dazzlingly intelligent man became a shell and his wisdom died before he did. He ended up as a sad, weak, foolish old man, whose kingdom fell apart during the reign of his son, but the consequences of this weakness lived on and grew to disastrous proportions.

"The problem is that once you introduce idol worship into a community, it is virtually impossible to root it out. The villagers liked it. It gave them pleasure to think that wild sexual spring orgies at the hill-shrines between and within whole villages had a religious significance.

32   1 Kgs. 11:7-33.

These practices took root in northern Israel, but on a smaller scale in Judah. However, you can tell how deep it went when a couple of generations later King Asa of Judah actually deposed his queen mother Maacah from her place in court for worshiping at an Asherah pole.[33] She was a granddaughter of Absalom by the way. Not only are these ways cruel, for example in the practices of pagan sacrifice, or the forced use of poor girls and boys as prostitutes in the pagan temples, but with it people also lose their minds and their judgment. Add to this the violent oppression of the poor through slavery and you have a people who had thrown away their very humanity."

"Look at the history of Judah and you will find some very good, serious kings who cared for their people, but it was interspersed with periods of apostasy, followed by occasional revivals where a particular king would attempt to suppress the hill-shrines. Once Solomon had died, the ten northern Tribes, who called themselves the Kingdom of Israel, broke away from Judah and Benjamin in the time of Rehoboam, the son of Solomon. The northern Israelite kings were little more than local warlords. The first, Jeroboam, immediately introduced the golden calves of Dan to force an official break with the Temple in Jerusalem. Omri, the builder of Samaria, was the most powerful of all these kings. His son Ahab compounded these sins by marrying the formidable Jezebel, the daughter of the King of Tyre. She was a vicious woman who brought from Tyre a militant and malignant form of Ba'al worship[34] – her priests were everywhere. Despite her bloody end, and Elijah's triumph,[35] Ba'al worship was embedded too deeply to be stamped out, despite warnings by various prophets."

"There is the story of the prophet Hosea who was commanded to take a wife, Gomer, and have children. She then left him and became a common prostitute, falling into such desperate straits that she appeared for sale in the slave market, where Hosea bought her back. The purpose of the story was to illustrate the spiritual adultery of Israel

---

33 2 Chron. 15:16.

34 The Ba'al of Tyre was called Melquart.

35 1 Kgs. 18.

and the boundless love of our God for his sinful people. Unfortunately it had gone too far. Their idolatry and oppressive attitudes were like weeds infesting the crops. However much you try to pull them up, they grow and grow and eventually choke everything around them. Isaiah spoke about it in his poem 'The Song of the Vineyard'."

> Let me sing for my beloved my love-song concerning his vineyard:
> My beloved had a vineyard on a very fertile hill.
> He dug it and cleared it of stones, and planted it with choice vines;
> he built a watchtower in the midst of it,
> and hewed out a wine vat in it
> and he looked for it to yield grapes, but it yielded wild grapes.
>
> And now, O inhabitants of Jerusalem and men of Judah,
> judge between me and my vineyard.
> What more was there to do for my vineyard,
> that I have not done in it?
> When I looked for it to yield grapes, why did it yield wild grapes?
>
> And now I will tell you what I will do to my vineyard.
> I will remove its hedge, and it shall be devoured;
> I will break down its wall, and it shall be trampled down.
> I will make it a waste; it shall not be pruned or hoed,
> and briers and thorns shall grow up;
> I will also command the clouds that they rain no rain upon it.
>
> For the vineyard of the LORD of hosts, is the house of Israel,
> and the men of Judah are his pleasant planting;
> and he looked for justice, but behold, bloodshed;
> for righteousness, but behold, an outcry! (Is. 5:1-7)

"In my youth, the worship of idol deities had become so much a part of daily life that it was thought of as normal practice. Jeremiah made it plain that Judah had become worse than the exiled ten tribes of northern Israel. Traditionally they had looked down on these tribes as ignorant country folk, so when the Assyrians under Sennacherib swept west about two centuries ago and trampled all over them, the Judahites took the callous attitude 'serve them right'. Here in Babylon we think of the three deportations of the people of Judah if we count those youths, including Daniel, who were taken first to Babylon. However, the ten tribes were deported two hundred years ago by the Assyrians to the area around Gozan (east of Haran) and some of the cities in Media. No one knows what ultimately has become of them. Deportations are never gentle and many probably died on the way."

"Jeremiah pleaded with the people of Judah over this very matter."

> The LORD said to me in the days of King Josiah: "Have you seen what she did, that faithless one, Israel, how she went up on every high hill and under every green tree, and there played the whore? And I thought, 'After she has done all this she will return to me,' but she did not return, and her treacherous sister Judah saw it. She saw that for all the adulteries of that faithless one, Israel, I had sent her away with a decree of divorce. Yet her treacherous sister Judah did not fear, but she too went and played the whore. Because she took her whoredom lightly, she polluted the land, committing adultery with stone and tree. Yet for all this her treacherous sister Judah did not return to me with her whole heart, but in pretence." (Jer.3:6-10)

"To be considered worse than the Ten Tribes was an insult to the sophisticated Jerusalemites, as indeed it was meant to be. Ba'al worship was considered a shameful thing.[36] From our youth this shameful thing devoured all for which our fathers had once laboured, their flocks and their herds, their sons and their daughters. We should have lain down in our shame, and let dishonour cover us for we refused to obey the voice of the LORD our God. However, what father has not pleaded with errant children to return to Him?"

---

36   "Ba'al, god of shame" is a play on words in Hebrew.

"You will have heard of Sennacherib of Assyria and his attempted siege of Jerusalem? How he was held off by Hezekiah, King of Judah? Given the fearsome reputation of the Assyrians, that was an immensely brave thing to do. It was an act of not only great physical courage but spiritual courage too. It looked as if that was a turning point. Judah had escaped by a miracle from the LORD. Her people seemed grateful and appeared open to moving in the right direction. But then Hezekiah's son, Manasseh, wrecked everything. He was a libertine of libertines who hated the traditional piety. He slew the prophets of the LORD, including Isaiah whom he sawed in two, and reintroduced every idol and abomination into the Temple and the altars at which they were worshipped. He dealt directly in witchcraft using mediums and necromancers, and even sacrificed his own children by burning. Manasseh reigned for 55 years and sealed Judah's future. He spent some time as a prisoner of the Assyrians but having repented of his evil he was eventually restored to his throne.[37] After this he semi-restored the Temple, but fifty years of damage had been done and could not be easily undone. He was the worst King that Judah had ever had, not only for the things he did but also for the destruction he wreaked on the fabric of Judah. Restoring the Temple alone could not undo the damage that he had done to the attitudes of the populace. His son Amon repeated the sins of his father, but he was assassinated by his servants after just two years. The grandson, a young Josiah, took his place. What a Kingdom to have inherited! His reforms were doomed from the beginning."

"Once we were young," said Baruch with a raised, questioning eyebrow at Nebuzaradan, "yet we can recall that far back. When we were young we genuinely hoped that Josiah's reforms would take hold. The young always think that whatever is great in their eyes will naturally sweep the land and become the norm. It rarely happens. For a while we thought the reforms might stick, but then they fizzled out and died. As we have heard, Josiah was wholly genuine in his desire to turn his Kingdom back to the LORD but, however hard he tried, the rot had gone too deep and the weeds had overgrown everything."

---

37 2 Chron. 33:10-13.

"My Lord Nebuzaradan was correct. On orders from the King, soldiers raided the shrines, knocked over the sacred stones, cut down the hilltop groves and executed a few priests who fought back. The rest melted away and were hidden by the villagers, only to re-appear later. It turned out to be a superficial reform at best and, at worst, no reform at all. After he died they went back to their evil ways. The fact is that people were just too far gone. They had become true pagans. The remnant of those faithful to the LORD were ignored and even persecuted."

"It was during that decade before the Great Siege when they completely lost their moral compass. Instead, they listened to the caressing talk of false prophets and the wild predictions of pagan priests, all of which led to warped thinking. Each time Jeremiah gave warnings not to turn to Egypt for a false political solution it was as if a red mist fell over their minds and they became determined to do the opposite. Jeremiah was not the only one saying this. Have you heard of the prophet Zephaniah?"

There was a collective shaking of heads in the room.

"He was older than us but we knew him in our youth. I do not know what became of him. His name has disappeared into the abyss that has befallen us since his time. He was open and scathing of the habits of our people and did not hold back."

Woe to her who is rebellious and defiled, the oppressing city!
She listens to no voice; she accepts no correction.
She does not trust in the LORD; she does not draw near to her God.
Her officials within her are roaring lions;
her judges are evening wolves that leave nothing till the morning.
Her prophets are fickle, treacherous men; her priests profane
what is holy; they do violence to the law.
The LORD within her is righteous; he does no injustice;
every morning he shows forth his justice;
each dawn he does not fail; but the unjust knows no shame.
(Zeph. 3:1-5)

"Sadly, all the warnings of the prophets fell on deaf ears. Judah had turned her back on the LORD for two generations and had lost her bearings. When the time came to face the wolf-pack, she had lost her ability to think straight or even think at all. King David's reign began so well with such joy and hope but the tale of the two baskets of figs told to us by Baruch earlier has come true. The bad figs were destroyed at the Siege while the good figs are here in Babylon. The darkness of night has closed in around us and I do not yet see a glimmer of a new dawn on the distant horizon but it will come. The seventy years must end at some point."

8

THE GREAT SIEGE:
BUILDING HOPES
UPON MOONBEAMS

"Have you ever experienced the smell of a city under a long
siege?" asked Nebuzaradan, sweeping his hand around the
rest of the room.

"The stink of it drifts on the wind more than fifty miles away. If
the siege has been long and the city large, there will be thousands of
rotting bodies. In Jerusalem, half the population died of the plague
or of plain starvation. When the citizens tried to tip a body over the
wall, as often as not we would sling it back over the low parts of the
city walls. Then there were the rats by the thousand, who grew fat on
the putrefying bodies and vultures by the thousand. Add to this rich
mix the smell of the living cooped up for months and years and you
have an unbearably overpowering odour that soaks into the skin and
clings to every piece of clothing. For the besieging army the smell that
lingers around any army camp, such as from the latrines, is partly
masked by the heavy wood-smoke from the thousands of fires burning for months for warmth and food. Jackals would prey around its

perimeter sniffing out left over pickings. For those within the city it must have been torture. How they bore it and allowed Zedekiah's faction to hold out for so long against us is a mystery. He and his circle must have hoped that we would get fed up and go home, but to give up was not in Nebuchadnezzar's character. He had many faults but lack of tenacity was not one of them. He would always become enraged at being defied."

"The next thing you notice after the smell is the lack of trees. They were all cut down for fuel and general use. One major siege can destroy a country for a generation. The area from the coast and up to and around Jerusalem, and then up the Jordan Valley and onward further north into Lebanon had become a wasteland, denuded of trees and greenery and trampled by tens of thousands of feet. All the forests have been destroyed, including those of Gilead on both sides of the Jordan, and those of the Negev. We had patrols out to the coast, north to Lebanon and south to Sinai watching for the Syrians and the Egyptians but we also had foraging parties looking for food and for wood. We would rotate our units in and out, part of the time in the siege-line and part out on patrol, particularly the cavalry who needed fodder and exercise. Once Israel, Judah and beyond had been stripped, we imported food and wood on ships through Gaza and Joppa. If you had seen it, you would not have believed that Judah and Israel had once been countries luxuriating in foliage. There had been only a partial recovery from the Assyrian destruction of Samaria and their siege of Jerusalem a century and a half before. Every farmer knows instinctively that less vegetation means less rain and it was clear that the rains failed so much more often after those events, leading to an even greater loss of greenery. Drought is always the greatest fear – drought and locusts. By the time we had finished, it was a wasteland. Now it is likely to be worse. Unless the land is farmed carefully the weeds and briars proliferate during the regrowth, choking everything else and making it worse than a desert."

Eleazar, unable to contain himself, broke in with a question. "We cannot understand what King Zedekiah was thinking?"

Baruch took up the story. "You have to go back ten years earlier than this[38] and even before. Jehoiakim was the second son of Josiah but his religious inclinations were not those of his father. He had been heavily idolatrous, with all the trappings, so he had little time for Jeremiah and his message.[39] Not for him the zealous reforms of his father. He was a vain, selfish, political opportunist who vacillated between Egypt and Babylon."

Nebuzaradan broke in again: "The dominant court faction in Jerusalem clearly believed that Egypt would aid them. Also there were idolatrous Judahite communities living there. They were building their hopes on moonbeams. After their defeat by us at the battle at Carchemish,[40] Egypt was never capable of mounting a big enough campaign, even if they had been willing.[41] Babylon was now the great power of the region. However, the Egyptians loved to play games by promising much but delivering little. Our invasion around the time of King Jehoiakim's death ought to have thoroughly disabused them of this,[42] but we later learned that they still continued their tricks. Your second and much bigger deportation came at this point: your prophet Ezekiel was one of these."

"Yes, you are correct," said Baruch. "Jeremiah warned of the outcome. In Jehoiakim's fourth year this word came to Jeremiah from the LORD."

> Take a scroll and write on it all the words that I have spoken to you against Israel and Judah and all the nations, from the day I spoke to you, from the days of Josiah until today. It may be that the house of Judah will hear all the disaster that I intend to do to them, so that everyone may turn from his evil way, and that I may forgive their iniquity and their sin. (Jer. 36:1-3)

---

38   597 BCE.

39   Jer. 26:20; 9:26.

40   605 BCE.

41   2 Kgs. 24:1.

42   597 BCE.

"Then Jeremiah asked me to write on a scroll, at his dictation, all the words of the LORD that he had spoken to him, and said this:"

> I am banned from going to the house of the LORD, so you are to go, and on a day of fasting in the hearing of all the people in the LORD's house you shall read the words of the LORD from the scroll that you have written at my dictation. You shall read them also in the hearing of all the men of Judah who come out of their cities. It may be that their plea for mercy will come before the LORD, and that everyone will turn from his evil way, for great is the anger and wrath that the LORD has pronounced against this people. (Jer. 36:4-5)

"So I did all that he ordered me to do about reading from the scroll the words of the LORD in the LORD's house. Then a group of officials reported the event to the King who took the scroll and asked one of his officials, Jehudi, to read it to him. After a few minutes the King cut off a length of the scroll with a knife and burnt it on the fire. He continued in this manner until it was all gone, despite protests from three of his officials. The sad thing was that he did not turn a hair while he was doing it. The listening and then the burning were a ritual public rejection of the word of the LORD. Then he ordered our arrest but we went into hiding. This was a son of Josiah, you understand, who must have been turning in grave."

Nebuzaradan continued with an impassioned wave of the hand. "Jehoiakim belonged to that generation whose members were ignorant of the world beyond their own borders. He just did not understand, or want to understand, the sheer scale of the numbers stacked against him. He and his followers thought they could do as and when they wished without any consequences. When he died and his eighteen year old son Jehoiachin inherited the throne, it must have been one of Nebuchadnezzar's biggest mistakes to deport the boy here and place his uncle Zedekiah on the throne as his puppet.[43] Zedekiah was even vainer, more ignorant and selfish than his brother Jehoiakim.

---

43   2 Kgs. 24:17.

How did a king as godly as Josiah produce such sons? Zedekiah was weak, always ready to veer with the wind and listen to and agree with whichever voice had last whispered in his ear. Nebuchadnezzar had not realised this and so he took Zedekiah's fawning and grinning protestations of eternal fealty as a set of definitive promises. Zedekiah might have meant what he said at the time but, as ever, he shifted with the wind, so once Nebuchadnezzar had returned home to Babylon, the deluded Egyptian court faction in Jerusalem then regained their dominance over him. In their eyes, Egypt was the ultimate power, but they believed this out of ignorance. They knew next to nothing of Babylon, Persia, Media and Elam. Moreover, given your history, the irony of turning back to Egypt for help was lost on them."

"In the intelligence service we knew almost everything that was going on inside Zedekiah's circle: every word, every stratagem, and every fear. Not a flea could have bitten them without us knowing. We knew immediately that Zedekiah was one big mistake, but our influence with the King was limited. One of Nebuchadnezzar's characteristics was that he would often ignore the advice of his ministers. We also knew all about Jeremiah and his prophecies, although, at the time, I did not understand their origin. At that early stage, I thought they were just the ramblings of a man who felt himself to be in touch with yet another god. It was only later that I began to understand."

"Egypt had been meddling again and had sent forces into Judah and further north, which had persuaded the Jerusalem court that Egypt was the real power. Egypt had deluded them into thinking that they would stay and protect them, although I wonder if there was also an element of self-delusion, even when the Egyptian forces withdrew. The court thought the Egyptians would always come back and fight us off – we knew better. Nevertheless, they instituted a reign of terror over their own populace to keep them in line."

"When our inside information confirmed as an established fact that Judah had broken with Babylon, Nebuchadnezzar went ballistic. He decided on a full-scale invasion with no other orders but to besiege and take the city at whatever cost and however long it took. At any stage, if Zedekiah had decided to change course and honour his sworn fealty to us, Nebuchadnezzar would have been happy. He was used to the poisonous faction fighting, deadly rivalries, temporary alliances and switches of allegiance of the Babylonian court. All that was normal life to him, the warp and weft of daily court life, but he would not tolerate outright defiance. He was the Great King, the Head of Gold, and no-one, but no-one, had the right to defy him!"

Baruch spoke again: "Looking back, Zedekiah was never capable of changing course. He was a virtual puppet prisoner of that court faction. In fact, he was always someone's puppet. He was a sad man and in his weakness he had allowed his people to sleep-walk into disaster. Despite warnings from Jeremiah[44] he had been unable to prevent intrigue with Egypt among the ruling families who were constantly urging rebellion in alliance with the new Pharaoh Hophra.[45] The obsession with Egypt among the leading families was so strong that they tightened their reign of terror against the population to keep them from surrendering once the siege began."

"You might ask yourself why it was not obvious to them that they would lose this war. With the virtue of hindsight, they could never have won, yet it did not seem so to them at the time. Initially, what encouraged the defenders was the common knowledge that Jerusalem was a hard city to besiege, not only because of the way it is positioned with ground sloping below the walls on three sides, but because of its internal water source, the Gihon spring. Without that spring of water there would be no city at all, not that high up in the mountains. For a major city it is unique. Everyone knew of the tunnel that King Hezekiah had dug through the rock at the time of the Assyrian invasions to divert the water into the city.[46] The siege was prolonged by both this and the fact that they had prepared for it in advance with great stores of food. Nebuchadnezzar waved his hands and gave the orders, but we knew we were in for a very long slog."

---

44   Jer. 37:6, 38-1.

45   589 BCE.

46   2 Chron. 32:30.

"Jeremiah consistently urged the policy of surrender[47] but the court was having none of it. Firstly, they had the pagan priests mumbling nonsense in their ears. Then the false prophets of the LORD weighed much greater in the balance than Jeremiah. All opinion was against him and his prophecies despite the fact that he was the only one who turned out to be right. The received opinion was that we Babylonians would either get bored, give up and leave, or the Egyptian army would appear and drive us off. It was not only a delusion but one that had become so entrenched that they refused to consider anything else. Once back in Egypt their army never even left their quarters but, if they had, they could not have even reached Gaza. We not only had had their measure but we also had many troops positioned on the coastal route from Sinai ready to block such a move."

Turning to Nebuzaradan, Baruch said: "Were you aware that Jeremiah and I tried to leave the city? We were stopped and he was arrested for treason. That was when they threw him into that cistern with mud at the bottom." Then he started to quote, from the depths of his memory, the text that he had once written:

Now Shephatiah the son of Mattan, Gedaliah the son of Pashhur, Jucal the son of Shelemiah, and Pashhur the son of Malchiah heard the words that Jeremiah was saying to all the people: "Thus says the LORD: He who stays in this city shall die by the sword, by famine, and by pestilence, but he who goes out to the Chaldeans shall live. He shall have his life as a prize of war, and live. Thus says the LORD: This city shall surely be given into the hand of the army of the King of Babylon and be taken." Then the officials said to the King, "Let this man be put to death, for he is weakening the hands of the soldiers who are left in this city, and the hands of all the people, by speaking such words to them. For this man is not seeking the welfare of this people, but their harm." King Zedekiah said, "Behold, he is in your hands, for the King can do nothing against you." So they took Jeremiah and cast him into the cistern of Malchiah, the King's son, which was

47   Jer. 21:1; 34:1; 37:3; 38:1.

in the court of the guard, letting Jeremiah down by ropes. And
there was no water in the cistern, but only mud, and Jeremiah
sank in the mud. (Jer. 38:1-6)

"I thought he was gone, almost certainly drowned in the thick mud at
the bottom of the cistern. I think he did too, for he later said to me
that he had sunk up to his armpits. I did not suffer the same fate as
they had put me in the guardhouse, so I could do nothing and knew
nothing until afterwards. Help came from the eunuch Ebed-Melech,
however, who raised the matter with the King. Ever suggestible,
Zedekiah gave orders for Jeremiah to be pulled up, but then the next
event shows how much he himself was a prisoner of the dominant
court faction. This is what Jeremiah said to him."

Thus says the LORD, the God of hosts, the God of Israel: "If you
will surrender to the officials of the King of Babylon, then your
life shall be spared, and this city shall not be burned with fire,
and you and your house shall live. But if you do not surrender to
the officials of the King of Babylon, then this city shall be given
into the hand of the Chaldeans, and they shall burn it with fire,
and you shall not escape from their hand." (Jer. 38:17-18)

"The King then said to Jeremiah, 'I am afraid of the Judahites
who have deserted to the Babylonians, lest I be handed over to them
and they deal cruelly with me', to which Jeremiah responded:"

You shall not be given to them. Obey now the voice of the LORD
in what I say to you, and it shall be well with you, and your life
shall be spared. But if you refuse to surrender, this is the vision
which the LORD has shown to me: Behold, all the women left in
the house of the King of Judah were being led out to the officials
of the King of Babylon and were saying:

'Your trusted friends have deceived you and prevailed
against you;

now that your feet are sunk in the mud, they turn away from you.'

All your wives and your sons shall be led out to the Babylonians, and you yourself shall not escape from their hand, but shall be seized by the King of Babylon, and this city shall be burned with fire. (Jer. 38:20-23)

"Then Zedekiah told Jeremiah this."

Let no one know of these words, and you shall not die. If the officials hear that I have spoken with you and come to you and say to you, "Tell us what you said to the King and what the King said to you; hide nothing from us and we will not put you to death," then you shall say to them, "I made a humble plea to the king that he would not send me back to the house of Jonathan to die there." Then all the officials came to Jeremiah and asked him, and he answered them as the King had instructed him. So they stopped speaking with him, for the conversation had not been overheard. (Jer. 38:24-28)

"We both remained in the court of the guard until the day that Jerusalem was taken. As you can imagine, we had little to eat but more than those poor souls left to fend for themselves in the city."

"Soon after a breach was made and the Babylonian army forced an entry. The defenders were weak, exhausted and small in number. It was all over in a matter of hours. True to his character, Zedekiah escaped by way of the King's garden through the gate between the two walls and fled. It was typical that he abandoned his people to the wrath of their enemies."

Nebuzaradan broke in here: "Besieging a city is a long game. There are the usual strategies. First we probed the weak points such as the gates, then we attempted a full assault using scaling ladders. The gates were too strong and the sloping ground on three sides up to the walls made scaling almost impossible and the wall on the north side was too strong. If besieged for long enough, cities will often surrender by negotiation at some point. However, in this case we knew from our extensive inside knowledge that this was not likely to happen because the ruling faction were still banking on Egypt marching to their rescue. Finally, we brought in our engineers. It can take weeks or even months to undermine a wall by digging down and then under, while needing elaborate protection from the defenders above. Only then can the engineers start the process of levering the big stones out one by one. We made extensive preparations the night before the last stones were to be removed."

"Once the breach was made the next day, it was soon over. We had too many men and once through the wall and into the city it was clear how weak the defences were. Zedekiah and his band fled by way of the King's Garden through the gate between the two walls, but we pursued them and overtook them in the plains of Jericho. Our cavalry was fresh while theirs was weak and relatively few in number. We brought Zedekiah up to Nebuchadnezzar, who was waiting at Riblah, in the land of Hamath[48] and there he passed sentence on him. Nebuchadnezzar was in no mood for mercy. He slaughtered the sons of Zedekiah at Riblah before his eyes, and then he slaughtered all the nobles of Judah. Then he put out Zedekiah's eyes and bound him in shackles to take him to Babylon. He was a pathetic sight and did not last long. He was a sad case."

Baruch said, "The siege may have been over but the next phase of the story was already about to unfold."

---

48   On the Lebanese-Syrian border.

CHAPTER

9

THE GREAT SIEGE: THE AFTERMATH

The kings of the earth did not believe,
nor any of the inhabitants of the world,
that foe or enemy could enter
the gates of Jerusalem. (Lam. 4:12)

"There is only one thing worse than a siege and that's what happens at the point when the city has fallen," said Nebuzaradan. "It's worse than any nightmare you can imagine. My stomach heaves at the memory of it."

"Even though our men had been rotated in and out of the line for months, the ordinary soldiers among any set of besiegers suffer along with those among the besieged. Siege camps are rife with rats, dysentery, fevers and disease so the casualty rate is enormous. The latrine system we had attempted to dig was primitive in the extreme because of the rocky ground. Outside the city, apart from a few wells in the surrounding villages, there was very little water, except from that collected in stone-cut cisterns. One of Jerusalem's strengths was

its internal water system fed by the Gihon Spring, which meant we
had to ship water up to the city in skins by the thousand. The sheer
scale and the difficulty of the issues we faced just supplying our army
fuelled the hopes of those in the city that we would give up and go
away. Indeed, there were severe rumblings of discontent among our
men, and ill-discipline was growing. The longer the siege lasted the
more the men's fury against the defenders rose. They had been promised loot of gold, silver and precious stones and they were determined
to have their share. After we broke into the city through the breach
in the walls, the fighting was over quickly, in hours in fact. Despite
orders to the contrary, they ran out of control, killed every living thing
in their path, and then went on a rampage of destruction. The interior
of the city had been in a pitiable condition even before we broke in.
Death had stalked every street during the siege, but our men then
turned it into an abattoir, with blood flowing in rivers. Dismembered
and disembowelled bodies were scattered across every street. The pri-
mary order the senior commanders had been given was to chase down
Zedekiah and his little fleeing force. That only took a day. Once that
was achieved it took time to gain control over the men, but by then
the damage had been done."

"When I rode through the city I was aghast. Apart from our forces,
there was nothing left alive. There were heaps of bodies strewn everywhere and even more of those that had died before the breach and had
been left to rot for want of burial space. It was the most gruesome sight
imaginable, and I have seen some in my time. Everything movable had
been smashed in the search for loot or out of plain, wanton fury."

"I had given orders to a section of my men to secure the Temple,
its precincts and contents, and to attend to nothing else. They had
achieved this rapidly. Nebuchadnezzar had not yet decided what to
do with it but he had given specific instructions to the effect that
he wanted the remaining vessels of the Temple captured intact. You
will recall that the main set had been taken by Nebuchadnezzar ten
years before?"

"You do realise that they still exist? They were brought here after
their confiscation ten years before the Siege, as you must have known.

The King had them put in store. As far as I know, they are still here." A wry smile passed across Nebuzaradan's old face. "One day you might wish to reclaim them," he said drily.

"I had also given orders to another section of my men to secure Jeremiah and Baruch whom they found imprisoned in the guard-house. We knew they had been imprisoned but I was afraid that they might have been cut down by marauding soldiers on the rampage. I was glad to have found them safe."

"It turned out that the men who ran the Temple precincts, all the court officials and nobles who had run the reign of terror against the population and forced them to continue the siege, had deserted the city along with Zedekiah. By then they were being transported to Riblah in shackles. As you know, none of them survived the wrath of Nebuchadnezzar. I had little sympathy for them, which I reserved for the poor of the populace who had been left outside the city and who had been forced to work for us throughout. Together with Jeremiah and Baruch, they were the only ones to survive. They were a sad, starv-ing bunch, far too weak for the trench digging needed to bury the bodies. The poor starving wretches who had been terrorized within had been cut down in the slaughter."

"I was put in charge of the next and final step. I had specific orders from the King which I dared not disobey. The walls, palaces and main houses were to be demolished and the Temple was to be stripped and then burnt. He wanted to eliminate Jerusalem com-pletely by just turning it into a heap of stones. The duplicity and defi-ance of her leaders had convinced him of the necessity of this but, in his fury, he wanted even more extreme measures. It amounted to the destruction of Judah as a kingdom by turning it into a pastoral back-water, incapable of rebellion ever again."

"People will fight for their culture and their way of life. You can wipe out part of a generation of people and burn their homes but the survivors will still come back. However, destroy the achievements of a people and their history and it is as if they had never existed. This was the reason for the destruction of the Temple which had stood for cen-turies as a symbol of everything that had set Judah apart from all the other nations. Apart from its beauty, in the eyes of the world it was a symbol of Judah's claim to have a unique Deity who had brought the world into existence, and had then chosen the Twelve Tribes of Israel and protected them. Nebuchadnezzar wanted no competition. He was the Head of Gold who brooked no equal on earth. That was why Babylon turned into a wild boar, trampling and goring all the surrounding nations."

"The walls, the palaces and the greater stone houses were the easy part. I had thousands of men from the Imperial Guard at my disposal and huge gangs of slaves. The smaller stones could be levered off the wall layer by layer with relative ease. The bigger ones could be shifted by ropes pulled by oxen and gangs of men. We pulled most of the walls down and left them in heaps. The other part, the destruction of the Temple, I did with a heavy heart. As I told you, I knew Jerusalem well from my earlier time during Josiah's reign and had been astonished and over-awed by the beauty of her Temple. I had learned slowly of its history and significance in your national life, even if many of your own people had ignored it, but there was no chance of pleading with the King. Some of the mercenaries in our army recruited from among the Edomites would stand around chanting:"

"Lay it bare, lay it bare, down to its foundations. (Ps. 137:7)

"They were gloating and gleeful at the fall of their ancient enemy, especially the Temple, even though their own lands would eventually be overwhelmed in Nebuchadnezzar's onslaught."

"Your ancestors in Josiah's time had done a partial job at restoration of the Temple after its closure and neglect during Manasseh's time but the bronze and gold metalwork was still exquisite. The pomegranates in the decoration were beautiful. The vessels, which were clearly more modern replacements of the set the King had confiscated ten years before, were sent back here to Babylon under close guard. It was decided that the pillars of bronze, the stands and the bronze sea contained too much valuable metal to leave behind, so the men broke it out with hammers and axes, carried it away in chunks and then melted it into ingots for ease of transport. Then they burned all the cedar pieces that had been overlaid with gold to melt it off. Then they burned the structure. The final result was just ash with a few burned stones. The old City of David has gone. I am not proud of the part I played, I assure you."

"The next step in my orders were to divide the poor remnant into two. Some were left as vine-dressers and local farmers. The King would still be demanding taxes and someone had to work the land to pay them! Poor souls, for it would have been an impossibly hard life. I then appointed a local official called Gedaliah to be the Governor. The rest of the people were to be deported here. Some of them might have been your parents or grandparents but there were not many of them. Few will have survived the journey."

"Finally I set Jeremiah and Baruch free, gave them some money and supplies and offered them a choice: either travel with me back to Babylon or stay. They chose to stay."

Baruch cut in here. "Jeremiah was in no shape to go anywhere and he and I were bound together by an unbreakable bond. When he saw the state of the city, which by now was no city at all, he was devastated. He was virtually prostrate with grief. The fact that he had predicted it all, and warned the people time and again made no difference. You know his Lamentations poetry?"

> How lonely sits the city that was full of people! How like a widow has she become, she who was great among the nations! She who was a princess among the provinces has become a slave. She weeps bitterly in the night, with tears on her cheeks; among all her lovers she has none to comfort her; all her friends have dealt treacherously with her; they have become her enemies. Judah has gone into exile because of affliction and hard servitude; she dwells now among the nations, but finds no resting place; her pursuers have all overtaken her in the midst of her distress. (Lam. 1:1-3)

"He would walk round the ruined city tears streaming down his face. He felt a kinship with the city and the people he loved. Its physical devastation and his emotional state became one, as if fused together, and he spoke as if his own emotions embodied those of the city:"

> I am the man who has seen affliction under the rod of his wrath;
> he has driven and brought me into darkness without any light;
> surely against me he turns his hand again and again the whole day long. (Lam. 3:1-3)

"During the short period while we were still prisoners, before our release, we had also seen the devastation of the land – just a wasteland as far as the horizon. It had been trampled and stripped by the besieging army. Jeremiah had once prophesied these words, which at the time I had taken to be a vision of the ends of the earth."

> I looked on the earth, and behold,
> it was without form and void;
> and to the heavens, and they had no light.
> I looked on the mountains, and behold,
> they were quaking,
> and all the hills moved to and fro.
> I looked, and behold, there was no man,
> and all the birds of the air had fled.
> I looked, and behold, the fruitful land was a desert,
> and all its cities were laid in ruins
> before the LORD before his fierce anger. (Jer. 4:23-26)

"Having seen Jerusalem and the surrounding land of Judah I wondered if that hell on earth had not arrived already and this was what he had meant."

"For a period he was almost deranged with grief to such a degree that I feared for his life. It actually felt worse than the siege itself and the opposition that had come before. For him, all the decades of prophetic warnings had come true in an even more gruesome way than even he had predicted. Because of the obduracy of the rulers and their reign of terror over the people they had given no thought to the consequences of defying Nebuchadnezzar."

> For the chastisement of the daughter of my people
> has been greater than the punishment of Sodom,
> which was overthrown in a moment,
> and no hands were wrung for her. (Lam. 4:6)

"During the siege there were terrible stories of cannibalism among the starving populace which persisted afterwards among the survivors."

> The hands of compassionate women
> have boiled their own children;
> they became their food
> during the destruction of the
> daughter of my people. (Lam. 4:10)

"But then he slowly began to recover, at least for periods of time. In the same passage we read:"

> Remember my affliction and my wanderings, the wormwood and the gall! My soul continually remembers it and is bowed down within me. But this I call to mind, and therefore I have hope: The steadfast love of the LORD never ceases; his mercies never come to an end; they are new every morning; great is your faithfulness. "The LORD is my portion," says my soul, "therefore I will hope in him." .... For the Lord will not cast off forever, but, though he cause grief, he will have compassion according to the abundance of his steadfast love; for he does not afflict from his heart or grieve the children of men. (Lam. 3:19-24; 31-33)

"But then he would break into heart-breaking pleas for restoration."

But you, O LORD, reign forever;
Your throne endures to all generations.
Why do you forget us forever,
Why do you forsake us for so many days?
Restore us to yourself, O LORD, that we may be restored!
Renew our days as of old – unless you have utterly rejected us,
And you remain exceedingly angry with us. (Lam. 5:19-22)

"We thought we were going to stay there with the remnant under Gedaliah at Mizpah, near Gilead. We had been joined by Ishmael, Johanan, the sons of Ephai the Netophathite, and all their men.[49] These were captains of groups of armed bands who had grown up everywhere, many of them deserters or escapees rampant around the countryside. They were marauding across the land in search of food and anything they could find. They were wild men, driven to utter desperation because there was nothing left to eat or loot. The Babylonian army had seen to that."

"Gedaliah was far too confident. He said 'Do not be afraid to serve the Babylonians. Dwell in the land and serve the king of Babylon, and it shall be well with you. I will dwell at Mizpah, to represent you. Gather wine and summer fruits and oil, and store them in your vessels, and dwell in your cities that you have taken.' We were then joined by other Judahite refugees from Moab, Edom and Ammon and surrounding places. It seemed like the faintest beginning of a new start, but then it all began to unravel. Johanan warned Gedaliah that the King of Ammon had sent Ishmael to assassinate him, but Gedaliah refused to be warned. He was over-confident and rejected the advice. Then Ishmael brought ten men with him on a visit and did indeed murder Gedaliah. He even murdered eighty men who had subsequently ridden in and then, following this, he set off to cross over to Ammon with all the people from Mizpah as captives, including ourselves."

"He was caught by Johanan and his men at Gibeon but Ishmael escaped across the Jordan. Then an odd thing happened. Having rescued us, they gathered us all together and discussed about leaving

---

49 These events are recorded in Jeremiah chapter 41.

for Egypt. They asked Jeremiah for a word from the LORD which duly came."

> Thus says the LORD of hosts, the God of Israel: If you set your faces to enter Egypt and go to live there, then the sword that you fear shall overtake you there in the land of Egypt, and the famine of which you are afraid shall follow close after you to Egypt, and there you shall die. All the men who set their faces to go to Egypt to live there shall die by the sword, by famine, and by pestilence. They shall have no remnant or survivor from the disaster that I will bring upon them. For thus says the LORD of hosts, the God of Israel: As my anger and my wrath were poured out on the inhabitants of Jerusalem, so my wrath will be poured out on you when you go to Egypt. (Jer. 42:15-18)

"Then they flew into a mighty rage and said 'You lie! The LORD has not spoken to you. Baruch has put you up to this!' It was clear that they had just not learned anything. It was leaning on Egypt all over again, repeating the previous grievous mistake."

"And so they took us all by force to Egypt. That was how we ended up there. It was a dreadful journey. We were, in effect, prisoners and Sinai had turned into a wasteland. We arrived in terrible shape in Tahpanhes. There came to be significant Judahite communities living in Migdol, Tahpanhes, Memphis, and in the land of Pathros.[50] The problem was that they were still idolatrous."

"It was at Tahpanhes that Jeremiah finally died, worn out by exhaustion and grief. I barely survived myself. It was a horrible and grievous end for him but, before he died, Jeremiah dictated this to me."

> Take in your hands large stones and hide them in the mortar in the pavement that is at the entrance to Pharaoh's palace in Tahpanhes, in the sight of the men of Judah, and say to them, thus says the LORD of hosts, the God of Israel: Behold, I will send and take Nebuchadnezzar the King of Babylon, my servant, and

50   Jeremiah chapter 44.

I will set his throne above these stones that I have hidden, and he will spread his royal canopy over them. He shall come and strike the land of Egypt, giving over to the pestilence those who are doomed to the pestilence, to captivity those who are doomed to captivity, and to the sword those who are doomed to the sword. I shall kindle a fire in the temples of the gods of Egypt, and he shall burn them and carry them away captive. And he shall clean the land of Egypt as a shepherd cleans his cloak of vermin, and he shall go away from there in peace. (Jer. 43:9-12)

"We lasted hand to mouth for some years until finally the Babylonian army arrived under Nebuchadnezzar to harry Egypt. The Egyptian Pharaohs had always had a taste for conspiracies that meddled in the affairs of other nations without giving them any proper support. They had talked big and offered much but had ultimately given nothing. The dominant Jerusalem court faction had counted on them and had been badly let down. This was the result – a destroyed Judah whose exiles had fled to Egypt, only to be chased down by the Babylonian army."

"The Babylonians were looking for us with vengeance in mind. Even if they were innocent of the murder of Gedaliah themselves, in Babylonian eyes this remnant had fled and joined the enemy afterwards. They were in no mood for mercy and they showed none. We were half-dead from hunger and thirst anyway. It was as my lord Nebuzaradan described earlier. I recognized him and called out to him when they captured us. I thought I was finished but it turned out that on top of chasing the Judahite remnant, he was also looking for me. He already knew of Jeremiah's death. He recognized me and brought me here. As predicted, my life has been saved each time, but nothing more. That is why you find me here."

10

ONE LAST GLASS OF WINE

There were tears in the eyes of everyone in the room. Some were openly weeping, shocked at the story they had heard. "There are some things that are too hard to bear," thought Boaz in his grief, "yet Baruch has born it for decades. How has he been able to silently carry the terrible burden of this story for so long?"

Nebuzaradan spoke to the whole room: his tone was almost stern. "From your Scriptures I have learned the meaning of the words repentance and mercy. Those things in which I took part I cannot deny. Even though I acted under orders, I chose to obey them willingly. Initially, in my first posting, Jeremiah was just a young prophet of a foreign god but, over the decades after the siege, I began to realize that everything he had predicted had come to pass. As Baruch has already said, he could not have constructed it all himself. I consulted much with Daniel who found someone to help me with my written Hebrew. Through him I have read your Scriptures and learned the history of your people. I have come to realize that the LORD is real and that it is He who governs the kingdoms of men. I willingly bow down and acknowledge his hand in all this. Baruch and I have been but servants in a much greater affair. Nevertheless, nothing can compensate for the damage I caused your people, because I played a major part in the great whirlwind of evil that has arisen out of Babylon's conquests. I will have to stand before the LORD under judgment for what I have done, but I also learned from Daniel that His mercy is everlasting. In my repentance I am counting on this."

"You have been set a monumental task. Babylon drove its armies through other lands like a wild boar, trampling and plundering them and then subjugating them to its will solely for the greater glory of Nebuchadnezzar. Your responsibility now, in this generation, is to follow the LORD with all your heart and soul. Baruch has already read Jeremiah's words about the seventy years."

> When seventy years are completed for Babylon, I will visit you, and I will fulfil to you my promise and bring you back to this place. For I know the plans I have for you, declares the LORD plans for welfare and not for evil, to give you a future and a hope. Then you will call upon me and come and pray to me, and I will hear you. You will seek me and find me, when you seek me with all your heart. I will be found by you, declares the LORD and I will restore your fortunes and gather you from all the nations and all the places where I have driven you, declares the LORD, and I will bring you back to the place from which I sent you into exile. (Jer. 29:10-14)

Nebuzaradan smiled at his audience wryly. "You were put here in Babylon for a purpose, to be built up and not pulled down, and it is through you that your people will have their future. You are the good figs in Baruch's story. How does that feel?"

Then he continued: "Whatever the seventy years means, our Empire here in Babylon will not stand for long. The Medes and Persians wax stronger by the year. When their turn comes, as it surely will, they may not continue our policy of deportation and devastation. Who wishes to possess a far flung Empire comprised of ruined, unproductive lands that ought to be farmed. After all, from where do taxes come? A future king may send you home. Are you ready for this event? If you really wish to go home then you will have to go through the privations of the travel and the rebuilding. For nearly forty years the land has been empty, apart from the local drifters and squatters. Have you any conception of the state in which we left it and the state it could be in now, with countless numbers of brambles and briars, blocked wells and ruined walls? It will be infested with the remnant of those wolves and jackals whose ancestors were originally attracted by the feast of bodies. Dismiss from your minds any romantic notion of re-building the nation in a short period of time. You are all city folk, unused to forced marches and hard labour. You will have to deal with bandits and hostile local officials – we make a special breed of those in Babylon and they exist in every empire. There is nothing left of Jerusalem but heaps of stones and overgrown fields with no stores of food, seeds or tools. You will have to start again and rebuild from the ground up. You may have to live out in the open for months or even years while you build your own houses. Most of you here are scribes. Are you ready for a different sort of work that could take generations? Think on what I am saying and consider how long and hard it will be to recreate a nation. If indeed you get the opportunity and you wish to take it, then may the LORD be with you."

"Now I fall back on the privilege of old age." His manner became more formal. "I thank you all for attending this meeting but now I am exhausted and wish for some peace. You must all be aching for your own beds. Baruch, would you stay for one last glass of wine with me?"

Jozadak the high priest rose, bowed, and said "Let us recite the Shema[51] together." The whole room, Nebuzaradan included, intoned:

Hear, O Israel: The LORD our God, the LORD is one. You shall love the LORD your God ...

The men had gone, filing out in varying degrees of tearful exhaustion. Boaz had been helping Baruch to rise but it was not clear who was helping whom. Even the young officer had gone, although he and the escort were no doubt close by outside.

---

51 This is poetic licence: we do not know when the recitation of the Shema began, or when it began to be called by that name, or when it became central to Jewish liturgy.

Nebuzaradan and Baruch were now alone. "So the deed is done, Baruch, and the story is out," said Nebuzaradan. "Indeed, I have waited many years for this night. We had to tell it sometime before it was too late, but I have one last question. The God of Israel, whom I now acknowledge as my God, had a purpose in calling Jeremiah and yourself to serve him. I spent a life serving Nabopolassar and Nebuchadnezzar, only to discover that the desperation to succeed of those who served them, including myself, was worthless. People drive themselves to an early grave to claim an illusion. What drives *your* people? Is it to obey Moses as an end in itself or is it something deeper? In my repentance I have learned that when God really guides us, the events through which it happens usually come unseen out of nowhere, but asking about his *greater* purposes leaves me with a blank mind."

"There has to be something more," persisted Nebuzaradan. "When the God of Israel called Abraham and set his line through Isaac, Jacob and the Twelve Tribes, followed by the Exodus to the Promised Land, it was surely for more than just 'obey me and all will go vaguely well with you but if you do not then you are in trouble'? I do not wish to trivialize these matters, but I suggest that there has to be a deeper purpose, an ultimate goal. There is a passage in Jeremiah's writings that says this."

Behold, the days are coming, declares the LORD, when I will make a new covenant with the house of Israel and the house of Judah, not like the covenant that I made with their fathers on the day when I took them by the hand to bring them out of the land of Egypt, my covenant that they broke, though I was their husband, declares the LORD. For this is the covenant that I will make with the house of Israel after those days, declares the LORD: I will put my law within them, and I will write it on their hearts. And I will be their God, and they shall be my people. And no longer shall each one teach his neighbour and each his brother, saying, 'Know the LORD,' for they shall all know me, from the least of them to the greatest, declares the LORD. For

> I will forgive their iniquity, and I will remember their sin no more. (Jer. 31:31-34)

"Did you understand it when he dictated it to you? What will this covenant be? How will he forgive their sin? There are also passages in Isaiah that speak of a time to come when all His people will live in peace together with Him. Is it a place or a land? If so, I want to reach this."

Baruch answered cryptically "There are many things I still do not understand, but Jeremiah also prophesied this:"

> And I will give you shepherds after my own heart, who will feed you with knowledge and understanding. And when you have multiplied and been fruitful in the land, in those days, declares the LORD, they shall no more say, "The ark of the covenant of the LORD." It shall not come to mind or be remembered or missed; it shall not be made again. At that time Jerusalem shall be called the throne of the LORD, and all nations shall gather to it, to the presence of the LORD in Jerusalem, and they shall no more stubbornly follow their own evil heart. (Jer. 3:15-17)

"Even Moses said that after himself there would come a prophet whose voice people should obey."

> The LORD your God will raise up for you a prophet like me from among you, from your brothers – it is to him you shall listen – just as you desired of the LORD your God at Horeb on the day of the assembly, when you said, "Let me not hear again the voice of the LORD my God or see this great fire any more, lest I die." (Deut. 18:15-16)

Baruch shivered slightly as a waft of a cool dawn breeze blew in through the window. "We have had many great prophets in our history but we have yet to see this one. Perhaps soon we will understand this mystery? Our time is close, very close, I can feel it. Then my friend, both of us will find out, but how long must Israel wait for his appearance? Now it is time to go." He suddenly raised his hand in a priestly gesture and intoned Aaron's Blessing over Nebuzaradan."

> The LORD bless you and keep you; the LORD make his face to shine upon you and be gracious to you; the LORD lift up his countenance upon you and give you peace. (Num. 6:24-26)

11

A FITTING END ...

It was the late evening of the day after. The elders were gathered again, together with Jozadak the High Priest, having spent much of the day resting. Emotional exhaustion and lack of sleep had enveloped them all. Their mood was sombre as each ruminated on what he had heard. The circle of people remained the same except for Boaz, the two old men at the centre of the story, and the young officer.

A household servant appeared and whispered to Eleazar and Jozadak. "Let him enter," was the response. Boaz entered the room. The dark rings under his eyes in his very pale face emphasized his youthfulness. He stood respectfully before Jozadak and Eleazar, and addressed them.

"Sirs, I bring you more urgent news. We went to awaken Baruch this afternoon, thinking him to be asleep, but we found him dead in his bed. He looked very much at peace. I volunteered to tell you the news."

They all bowed their heads in silence. They had known the old man just one day but the story he had recounted the night before made them feel as if they had known him for fifty years. He had carried silently in his breast the whole story of their people and now he was gone.

"So", said Eleazar, after a silence even longer than usual, "he has found his rest at last, after so much wandering and grief."

The household servant appeared yet again and whispered, this time in a more agitated fashion. In walked the same young officer of the night before. "Last night he was the precursor to an earthquake," thought Eleazar.

The young officer stood to attention before him. "Sir, I bring you news. My Lord Nebuzaradan died in his bed last night." A whisper of exhaled breath went around the room like the swish of wind in a wheat field. The young man looked faintly puzzled at the reaction. Eleazar then told him the news about Baruch. The officer sat down abruptly as his legs buckled under him. At last he spoke.

"I never told you my name. It is Baltazar. Nebuzaradan was my great grand-father. I am wholly grieved at his passing even though it has been anticipated for years. So many memories of my childhood lie with him. And now, after their momentous story, both men are gone in a single night, their lives forever intertwined. Their memories must have lain heavily upon them. Over the last weeks he impressed upon me a task he required me to do. His words were 'After I am gone you must continue to protect them. Promise me.' By this he meant your community. My family will endeavour to continue this."

CHAPTER

12

... AND A NEW BEGINNING

In the ten years that elapsed after 'that night', as he mentally referred to it, Boaz matured intellectually and physically. He grew from a very tall, awkward youth into a capable, well-mannered, big young man. Prepared by his mentor Itamar, the life that had been mapped out for him as a scribe had unfolded in a predictable fashion. Itamar himself had become visibly older and frailer, although he had lost none of his intellectual powers. Orphaned as a small child, Boaz had always looked up to him as the father he had never had and had taken over many of his scribal duties. Eleazar's committee also continued its slow, meandering course. The more pious among the Exiles lived an emotionally divided life between gradual assimilation into the crowded and dangerous fringes of Babylonian life while simultaneously suffering a deep yearning for a return to the land of Judah that gnawed away at their souls.

During that decade, other events had begun to unfold in distant lands. A King called Cyrus had appeared as the ruler of the Persian city of Persis[52] in a kingdom named Anshan. He had proceeded to conquer

---

52　This is generally referred to as the Achaemenid Empire.

his Median[53] overlord Astyages, whose daughter he had then married. Thereafter he had conquered and absorbed the Lydian Empire,[54] and had followed this with the conquest of Elam[55] and its capital Susa.

Although they were blissfully unaware of these events, only a few days after the defeat of Elam, Itamar called on Boaz to say that a meeting had been called for that evening. "I expect it to be just routine business where we are both required," he explained. Nevertheless, Boaz felt a strange sensation that something more important was in the wind. Perhaps it was the furtive whisperings in the market places that contributed to the strange atmosphere around the city? The meeting was in the same house as 'that night', before they had been escorted to Nebuzaradan's palace residence. The faces around the room were much the same and greeted him in familiar terms, for he had grown to know most of them very well over the intervening years. Eleazar announced that they were waiting for another visitor. To Boaz' astonishment, it turned out to be the young officer Baltazar, Nebuzaradan's great grandson, who had escorted them 'that night'. He had remained in that long nocturnal meeting and had re-appeared to announce his great-grandfather's death the next day. These events were forever etched in Boaz' mind. Baltazar too was greeted warmly by the scribes and leaders around the table. It was clear some form of bond had grown between them in those same intervening years. Boaz raised an eyebrow in Itamar's direction but received no response.

"The rumours flying round the markets about Cyrus are correct," said Baltazar. "We now have confirmation of his successful conquest of the Elamite Empire. It is almost certain that he will choose to press against us next and he is likely to make an attempt at the direct conquest of this city. It is not clear to me that we can stand against him if he makes an alliance with the Medes. Our once much vaunted army is now a shadow of its former self. However, this will take time – how long is hard to say – perhaps a year or two."

53 This conquest occurred in 550 BCE. At its greatest extent, the Median Empire stretched from eastern Turkey, through Persia to Afghanistan.

54 The Lydian Empire was located in the western part of modern Turkey.

55 The Elamite Empire, on the eastern side of the Persian Gulf, was conquered by Cyrus in 540 BCE.

The people in the room looked round in consternation. "I take it as read that what is said in this room tonight stays in this room? The reason for calling this meeting is to alert you well ahead of time to his likely attitudes if he does arrive. He does not seem to favour the Babylonian way of conquest, devastation and deportation. In those lands he has conquered so far, he has allowed exiled peoples to return to their lands if they wish. Therefore, you ought to ask yourselves what your attitude would be to a return to the land of Judah, if he succeeds. Of course, Cyrus may never arrive and you could accuse me of raising your hopes, but my own assessment is that it is more likely to happen than not. Apart from the potential devastation of a battle, will you be ready for your return? You cannot just walk out of the door and order a horse to take you back to Jerusalem. The journey will take months through possibly hostile territory, to reach a ruined land, empty except for vagrant dwellers. You will recall that my great grandfather gave you an eloquent warning about this a decade ago. That is why I am here, to provoke you into thinking and preparing for this in advance and offer you my help."

Itamar spoke up while the wheels were still clunking in Eleazar's mind. "We thank you warmly for this, my Lord. The question is how do we prepare? Most of us in this room have never even ridden a horse or trekked across country and we are too old to learn. We would not even know how to begin."

"I have well-trained, experienced men in my unit who are Judahites. I can assign some of them the task of teaching your younger men the arts of scouting and travelling, with additional weapons training. This can be done in an innocent manner without it being thought that rebellion is being prepared. Then these men can escort your people as they move back. A movement of even a small proportion of you will take a deal of time, money and preparation. These men have their own methods. It will be more about whom *they* choose rather than whom *you* choose. They know what to look for in a young man."

That was how Boaz found himself on periods away on camping trips, travelling out along the river, participating in what was innocently called 'Outdoor Torah Study'. He slept under tents made of skins, learned to light fires from carefully chosen brushwood, how to cook simple food and, to his initial disgust, gut and skin small animals. He found this life enjoyable and his legs became stronger with the exercise. Then slowly, over a period of weeks, he was taught to ride, initially on a mule and then a horse although, for his size, he needed a bigger animal than usual. It took him a while to learn how to sense the movement of the animal, guiding it by both bridle and legs so he and the horse were one. The most difficult part was the weapons training. He was not a naturally aggressive man so being attacked with a spear whose iron point has been replaced with a small leather ball was difficult for him. His instructor drilled him incessantly on how to be light on his toes, how to deflect full frontal thrusts, how to use the weapon to disarm an opponent and how to use the spear-shaft as a quarter-staff. Having spent the first few days on his back in the dust, he slowly began to catch on to the ideas as his reflexes improved. Finally, he reached the point where he could defend himself well. Next was sword-play, which he found less difficult as he had the advantage of height and reach. Having attained a basic competence in these matters he was then taught how to detach and re-attach a real spear-head, and then sharpen a sword, which brought home to him the possibility that one day he might be required to kill someone. Parrying an attacker with a spear or sword was one thing, but plunging his own weapon into their flesh was entirely another. He also worried that he might have to serve in the Babylonian army if Cyrus really did challenge the city.

After some weeks he was taken aside by one of the instructors, an older, squat man with a kindly face and manner. "Boaz", he said, "I have chosen you as my assistant."

Boaz was puzzled. "Why me, sir?" he asked. "Because you have excellent eyesight. You're alert and you also possess basic common sense. The elders know you and trust you. You are their representative, in a manner of speaking. Also, as a scribe you are qualified to teach," came the reply. "I have spent a lifetime travelling the routes along the Great River and I know all of them back to the lands of our fathers but my eyes are not so good these days. I need someone with me who can see properly across valleys and hills." It turned out that his name was Adar.

A year later, Cyrus turned his attention to the Babylonian Empire. The Persian and Median forces under him routed the Babylonian army in a battle near the riverside city of Opis[56] on the River Tigris, north of Babylon. The day when the dramatic news of the disastrous battle reached the city and consternation spread around its streets lived long in Boaz' memory. Then the survivors and casualties began to filter back and fill the city squares.

"Are we to expect a siege?" Boaz thought apprehensively. He looked up at the huge, thick walls with their great stones and remembered that evening when Baruch and Nebuzaradan had recounted the dreadful siege of Jerusalem.

The appearance of Cyrus and his army outside the great city walls also had consequences for Daniel. He was abruptly summoned out of retirement in a highly unusual way. Belshazzar, the effective day-to-day King of Babylon and son of King Nabonidus, made a great feast for a thousand of his lords and drank wine in front of them. He commanded that the vessels of gold and of silver that Nebuchadnezzar had taken out of the Temple in Jerusalem be brought before him. Belshazzar, together with his lords, wives and concubines wished to drink from them. These golden vessels were brought before him. The King, his lords, wives and concubines drank from them and praised the gods of gold, silver, bronze, iron, wood and stone.

Immediately the fingers of a human hand appeared and wrote on the plaster of the wall of the King's palace, opposite the lamp-stand. And the King saw the hand as it wrote. Then the King's colour changed, and his thoughts alarmed him; his limbs gave way, and his knees knocked together. The King called loudly to bring in the enchanters, the Chaldeans, and the astrologers. The King declared to the wise men of Babylon, "Whoever reads this writing, and shows me its interpretation, shall be clothed with

---

56   The Battle of Opis occurred in 539 BCE.

purple and have a chain of gold around his neck and shall be the third ruler in the Kingdom." Then all the King's wise men came in, but they could not read the writing or make known to the king the interpretation. (Dan. 5:5-8).

The King and his lords were greatly perplexed. The Queen told the King not to be alarmed because, in Nebuchadnezzar's time, there had existed a man called Daniel who had the gift of interpreting riddles and that "light and understanding and wisdom like the wisdom of the gods were found in him." She suggested that he be called. Then Daniel was brought in before the King. The King said to Daniel:

> You are that Daniel, one of the exiles of Judah, whom the King my father brought from Judah. I have heard of you that the spirit of the gods is in you, and that light and understanding and excellent wisdom are found in you. Now the wise men, the enchanters, have been brought in before me to read this writing and make known to me its interpretation, but they could not show the interpretation of the matter. But I have heard that you can give interpretations and solve problems. Now if you can read the writing and make known to me its interpretation, you shall be clothed with purple and have a chain of gold around your neck and shall be the third ruler in the kingdom. (Dan. 5:13-16)

What a way to be called out of retirement! Only Daniel could have uttered such an elegant rebuke and an interpretation so devastating:

> Let your gifts be for yourself, and give your rewards to another. Nevertheless, I will read the writing to the King and make known to him the interpretation. O King, the Most High God gave Nebuchadnezzar your father kingship and greatness and glory and majesty. And because of the greatness that he gave him, all peoples, nations, and languages trembled and feared before him. Whom he would, he killed, and whom he would, he

kept alive; whom he would, he raised up, and whom he would, he humbled. But when his heart was lifted up and his spirit was hardened so that he dealt proudly, he was brought down from his kingly throne, and his glory was taken from him. He was driven from among the children of mankind, and his mind was made like that of a beast, and his dwelling was with the wild donkeys. He was fed grass like an ox, and his body was wet with the dew of heaven, until he knew that the Most High God rules the kingdom of mankind and sets over it whom he will. And you his son, Belshazzar, have not humbled your heart, though you knew all this, but you have lifted up yourself against the Lord of heaven. And the vessels of his house have been brought in before you, and you and your lords, your wives, and your concubines have drunk wine from them. And you have praised the gods of silver and gold, of bronze, iron, wood, and stone, which do not see or hear or know, but the God in whose hand is your breath, and whose are all your ways, you have not honoured.

Then from his presence the hand was sent, and this writing was inscribed. And this is the writing that was inscribed: MENE, MENE, TEKEL, and PARSIN.[57] This is the interpretation of the matter: MENE, God has numbered the days of your kingdom and brought it to an end; TEKEL, you have been weighed in the balances and found wanting; PERES, your kingdom is divided and given to the Medes and Persians. (Dan. 5:17-28)

The news of the strange events occurring last night at the palace and the dramatic re-emergence of Daniel from retirement circulated the city like a fire out of control. Babylonians loved their gossip and this was the juiciest piece they had heard in years. Nevertheless, they were apprehensive over their future.

---

57 MENE and TEKEL sound like the Aramaic for *numbered* and *weighed* respectively, while PERES (the singular of *Parsin*) sounds like the Aramaic for *divided* and for *Persia*. See the footnotes in the ESV translation of Daniel.

Then the unexpected had happened. The soldiers of Gobryas, Cyrus' great general, diverted the River Euphrates into a canal dug previously as part of the defence system of the city. Their army then entered the city unopposed by simply walking along the riverbed. The unpopular King Nabonidus[58] and his son Belshazzar were deposed. The people gave the Persian troops a welcome. They wished to be left alone to get on with their lives.

Thus ended the Babylonian reign of terror. It was the beginning of the end of the Captivity.

58   Nabonidus was King of Babylon during 556-539 BCE.

CHAPTER

13

THE RETURN

The raised knoll near the head of the valley was covered by a thick vegetation of grass and dense bushes spread over its uneven surface. Boaz walked up its back and then burrowed into the vegetation and crawled up the last few yards, making sure his figure did not break the skyline. He found a place in which he could lie comfortably while simultaneously observing the valley in front and below him. The two horses were tethered out of sight at the base of the knoll, amiably munching on the sweet grass and attended by the boy who accompanied him. Boaz enjoyed days like these for he could both fulfil his duties as a scout while resting his weary, saddle-worn body. No longer the lean, callow boy of former years, his big, tall frame was beginning to fill out with muscle and his once dreamy face now had a wary, watchful look. The change in him had been gradual, yet there were times when he wondered how he came to be living this life, observing the movements in the valley below. In this peaceful, restful state lying in his bed of lush grass, his mind drifted back to the tumultuous excitement they had all felt when Cyrus had appeared in Babylon nearly a year ago.

The expectation that Cyrus would show a much greater degree of respect for the customs and religions of his conquered lands had turned out to be true. He had quickly ended the Babylonian policy of exile and deportation. What was the point of conquering lands and cities and then devastating them to such a degree that they were uninhabitable? Did he wish to rule over a wasteland? The city of Babylon itself and the other cities in its empire were swollen with exiled peoples, not least the people of Judah, who were pining to go home. Much better to send these people back to their respective provinces to rebuild and replant. They would show far greater loyalty this way than keeping them in subjection here. They would also yield taxes.

In fact, Cyrus went further. He had made a proclamation throughout all his kingdom and had also put it in writing:

> Thus says Cyrus King of Persia: The LORD, the God of heaven, has given me all the kingdoms of the earth, and he has charged me to build him a house at Jerusalem, which is in Judah. Whoever is among you of all his people, may his God be with him, and let him go up to Jerusalem, which is in Judah, and rebuild the house of the LORD, the God of Israel – he is the God who is in Jerusalem. And let each survivor, in whatever place he sojourns, be assisted by the men of his place with silver and gold, with goods and with beasts, besides freewill offerings for the house of God that is in Jerusalem. (Ez. 1:2-4)

Jeremiah's prophecy was fulfilled, thus giving him the last word.

The elation among the Exiles had been intense. With boundless enthusiasm, the great and the good among them had donated large quantities of silver, gold, horses, oxen and wagons by the score. It had taken some weeks for their elation to be tempered by the realization that the arduous and dangerous journey back to Judah could not be embarked upon lightly, nor was it clear how their return was to be organized. Indeed, there were some for whom life in Babylon had become a little too comfortable. They had put down roots and felt that the potential privations of the journey and the pioneering life were not for them. This step was for others to take first. They would consider it later when more was known. Under Baltazar's wise guidance, the elders had finally decided that those who wished to return would be divided into manageable ox-hauled wagon-trains, each train with its own independent transport carrying tools, weapons, clothing, seeds, and plantings, including herds of goats, sheep and cattle. Each train would be led by an experienced leader, one of Baltazar's men, who knew the route and the ways of the lands they had to cross. Boaz' group, led by Adar, was the vanguard heading for Jerusalem and would not be carrying full families of all ages. Apart from a few boys, they could not afford to carry children who were prone to illness, and might wander off without notice. They had to pick their people carefully to fit in with a window of time to make the journey, with no slack for delays. To Boaz' delight, the matriarch Deborah and her husband from the Residence were chosen to travel with them. She knew how to handle men and boys firmly, she knew how to cook in bulk and, moreover, she knew how to bargain and buy food in market places. They would have much bargaining to do along the way and it would have to be done with a good grace among peoples whom they did not wish to antagonize. Deborah's skills would be essential. Other trains would follow and head for their ancestral lands in the other towns of Judah, but their own train was meant for Jerusalem only. The prince Zerubbabel, together with the high priest Jeshua son of Jozadak, were to follow a few weeks after their vanguard had reconnoitred and secured the city. Full families would follow later. Boaz blessed Baltazar's far-sightedness and wisdom.

It had taken many weeks for the vanguard to get this far, trekking slowly through lands he had never known existed, populated by peoples whose languages were beyond him. Boaz was still young enough to enjoy these experiences and even yearn for more. His elder brethren were less enchanted. Oxen are slow at the best of times, moving at a dogged walking pace, but they showed their value in rough conditions where they could pull wagons over any rough ground or plough through boggy terrain. Most of the wagons were covered and doubled over as rough homes in which the Exiles slept and sheltered from the rain and sun. In his excitement and desire to return, Boaz found it all very tedious until his internal clock adjusted to the life

– so many rumbling leagues a day, eat, sleep and repeat. His own personal routine was more varied. His task was to ride out ahead to scout the ground, look for points in the land where ambushes by bandits could be laid, and report back to Adar. They were too big a group and too well-armed for this to be likely but it was better to be sure. They had been offered a military escort by the King but they had decided that to accept this was too timorous an act for a people who proudly claimed that the God of Heaven was with them. Ever cautious, Adar had organized a group of the younger men to act as a rear-guard – they did not want stragglers being picked off at a careless moment.

When not on guard duty, his nightly fireside chats with Adar slaked some of his thirst for the history of his own people. Adar had his own dry style of observation, honed by a lifetime in army camps. "My first memories were of a camp, somewhere, anywhere. I do not really recall any other life. Later I learned that there were thousands of kids like me and you, the orphans of war, sieges and epidemics from around the empire. You ended in the Residence and I in an army camp. I am older than you but I doubt by much, but I look much older because I have lived a lifetime in the open air and under the sun. The soldiers were generally kind and fed us from a big pot when there was food. When there was no food we starved like everyone else. As children the camp boys did the kitchen tasks necessary for living. When old enough we looked after the weapons and the teams of horses, camels and oxen. Then as we grew towards manhood we had proper training in all weapons and an absorption into the ranks. Soldiers have their own code of conduct and the camp was my life and schooling. There must have been hundreds of orphans from Judah, like me, among the even greater swathe from all the nations of the earth. I have fought and tramped over the whole empire."

"Eventually I rose to become a senior sergeant and that was how I came to be chosen by Baltazar. His great grandfather Nebuzaradan, whom I gather you have met, was one of the great ones at Court. You cannot go any higher than Captain of the Royal Guard. He was known by all of us as a formidable man, highly intelligent but not one to be crossed. He ran the Royal Guard as a separate elite unit and that is exactly what it was. He was one of the few trusted by Daniel when he administered the City and the empire. The two of them formed an alliance. The Royal Guard and the Army made it plain to the princes that they would not tolerate any conspiracies against Daniel. It was Daniel who taught Nebuzaradan the scriptures of our people. Even better, he taught him what they meant, and how to live by them."

"I have been thoroughly briefed about you Boaz so I know of your famous nocturnal meeting with Baruch and Nebuzaradan – that night has gone down in the lore of our people. Those months last year in the preliminary camps were spent checking you out to see if you had the physical strength and the eyesight to do what is necessary. There was no point choosing you if your sight was so bad that you would walk into a tree. As it stands, you will do very well. Now where were we? Yes, Nebuzaradan's eldest son is more of a routine administrator and not in the same league as his father. Baltazar the great grandson, however, has more of the force and intelligence of his great grandfather. Do not be deceived by his polite and polished manner. He's a force, I can assure you. A few years ago, although it seems like a lifetime now, I found myself being ordered to report to a senior officer. When I arrived it was Baltazar, whom I did not know from Adam. However, he had done his homework on me. He knew who I was, where I had served, my record, strengths and weaknesses but, to my surprise, he knew I was a Judahite. He came straight to the point: he explained who he was and that he had been present at that night's meeting. He explained, under an implied threat of secrecy, that he was there to recruit experienced Judahite soldiers with the ultimate aim of forming a trained escort for a future return to the lands of Judah."

Boaz laughed out loud. "What did you think at the time? Did you think he was crazy?"

"Oh, yes," chortled Adar, "but I was not going to contradict the great Nebuzaradan's great grandson, was I? I was also being paid very well, much better than before. After that it was not long before the rumours about Cyrus began to filter through and then I began to see what he was driving at. Talk about thinking ahead. He is as sharp as a newly whetted sword, that one. He obviously had all this planned out in advance and so now we are here!" He raised his vessel of beer and they drank to Baltazar.

They had been following the ancient trade-route along the Great River Euphrates for weeks in a north-westerly direction but now their train of wagons was about to swing to the west, south west. This was the reason he was lying where he was, hidden in the lush grass, observing the valley below. To pass through this was their next key objective as they ultimately headed for Tadmor and then the road to Damascus.

It was on this stage of the route during one of their evening fireside talks that Adar and Boaz had their first and only argument. As they turned away from the river the weather became much drier and hotter in the semi-desert environment. There was no lush grass here. Boaz had spent a lifetime next to the river and its accompanying breezes and he was not used to the dry, relentless heat that sapped his strength. One night, after a long day scouting in the sun, he had returned to camp in a state of exhaustion and dehydration that clogged his mind, leaving him distressed and unable to think. His body was also still adjusting to the physical exercise that he had lacked as a child in the Residence. His frustration at the incredibly slow plodding progress of the train boiled over in mild irritation as he muttered under his breath "Why are we doing this?" Adar rounded on him in a fury. "You know very well why we are doing this! We are going home to build a life. Do you really think that there is a place for us anywhere else in this accursed empire other than Jerusalem and Judah? You and I are the descendants of a temporarily useful remnant whom the Babylonians just wanted for our labour. The rest of our people perished and do not you forget it. Cyrus and his Persians might seem more enlightened, and so they are, but only up to a point. Do not be deceived. Once we cease to be useful to them they will discard us. When that happens we will get no protection and we will end up the prey of every head-case who imagines he has a grudge because once his great, great grandfather was dispossessed by your great, great grandfather. Empires always have exploited their myriad subject peoples. They always have and they always will. There will no doubt come a time when it will be politically expedient to sacrifice us and no-one will care. No-one wants us, so while we have their temporary attention and goodwill we are making our move. We have to fight to survive and we will be more successful concentrated in our own homeland than scattered everywhere else. I thought you understood this? Why have I been training you these last months?" Boaz could see that Adar was angry at his callowness and ignorance. He looked and felt duly crestfallen. Suddenly, with a look of concern, Adar said "Drink plenty of water and get some sleep. You look exhausted."

Lying under the stars that night, Boaz' tired body craved for sleep but his mind was alive in whirling activity under the lash of Adar's seemingly furious anger. He suddenly realised that until this moment he had possessed the attitude of a schoolboy scholar, always considering every matter from the abstract point of view, with the aim of gaining the approval of the elders. To reclaim and restore the Land had been the pillar on which he had been raised, but it had always been a high ideal, almost a theological tenet in his rigorously tutored mind. Now, for the first time, as the shell of his campfire romanticism fell away, reality had taken hold and he became acutely aware of the practical dangers that lay before them. The scale of the monumental task they had undertaken emerged from his subconscious. There was no room for failure – the Return was *now* and they had to succeed or die in the attempt. He began to comprehend why Adar had taken him through rigorous training in weapons, had taught him to ride a horse, light a camp fire, understand the lie of the land and even live off it if necessary, and finally to read tracks in the ground. At last he understood the need to be a responsible soldier and leader. Belatedly, the man was emerging from the chrysalis of the boy. Strangely, he felt comfortable with his new found self-knowledge and slowly drifted into sleep.

The next day he sought out Adar and apologized. "You were right, of course. I was just exhausted. I am just a beginner at this. I have not spent your time in the army marching, fighting and camping out in the open so I do not have your toughness of body and spirit.

The heat saps my will to struggle and survive. I am still getting used to it. Please give me time."

Adar's cheerful good nature had returned. "Not to worry. It will come in due course."

Their passing through Syria proved to be relatively uneventful. They fought off a few weak attacks by bandits who made half-hearted sorties against them. At one point Boaz found himself pitted against a ragged man with a rusty spear. He remembered his training and easily disarmed him with a deft twist and lift of his own spear. Boaz was relieved when the man ran away, saving him the unenviable task of wounding him. Otherwise, it was an uneventful journey. Cyrus had issued edicts about them on fancy scrolls to his provincial governors. This gave them protection, even a welcome, around the great and ancient cities such as Tadmor and Damascus. At Damascus they had to decide whether to head south westwards to the great fortress at Hazor, traversing the north end of Lake Kinneret and then later turn south to enter the north end of the old Northern Israelite Kingdom, or turn south immediately to Bosra and enter the Land south of Kinneret through Beth-Shan. Adar decided on the former. Taking the Beth-Shan route meant crossing the Jordan River, an easy matter in season for a small party, but a wagon-train pulled by oxen was a different story.

About a century and a half before the Exile, the ten tribes in the old Northern Kingdom based in Samaria had been defeated in battle and deported by the Assyrian Kings and replaced by others from the far-flung reaches of their sprawling empire. The new inhabitants of Samaria and northern Israel spoke not only Aramaic but a strange group of disparate languages, at least to Boaz' ear. Their hostility towards the home-bound Exiles increased once they became aware of the Judahite intention to rebuild and resettle Jerusalem. Cyrus was King in name in these far distant lands but no more than that. His edicts might be read by local governors and officials but Adar doubted whether they would be obeyed. His decision meant they had to run the gauntlet of these towns and villages all along Samaria. As they lumbered south they could sense the suspicion and hostility.

Their excitement rose to fever pitch when they finally reached Jerusalem lying at a higher altitude than they could have imagined. The ox-teams were exhausted after the final, agonizingly slow climb, so the decision was to camp early and reconnoitre at dawn, with extra guards posted for safety. More than a decade before, Nebuzaradan had warned them about the condition of the city and what they should expect to find there when they arrived. He had not exaggerated. He had also been right about the need to bring everything with them. The city and its surrounding towns and villages were in ruins, consisting of nothing more than piles of weed-infested stones, overgrown with thistles and brambles and haunted by wolves and jackals. Early the next morning, Boaz himself killed a wolf with his spear after it attacked him. The ravening wolf was fierce with sharp snarling fangs but his own visceral fear and the need for self-preservation arose within him as he drove his spear-point home hard into the body of the animal. He watched warily as the light died in its yellow eyes. It was his first blood. He discovered that he had no compunction in killing the wolf but the newly-awakened soldier in him also realized that from now on he would need to be doubly on guard.

After the incident with the wolf, Adar and Boaz wandered up Mount Moriah, the site of Solomon's Temple. There was no hint that one of the most beautiful buildings on earth had once stood there. In their zeal to obey Nebuchadnezzar's edict, and aided by gleeful, vicious Edomites, the Babylonian demolition teams had heaved most of the rubble down directly either into the Kidron Valley on the eastern side or down the Ophel on the tongue of land that stands in the south-south-westerly direction. The structured and carefully laid stonework of the walls of the City of David was nowhere to be seen. Nothing was left except a vista of rubble and weeds to the horizon. Even the fire-blackening of the remaining stone had been cleaned by fifty years of sun and rain. Boaz stood still in the clear, translucent light and cool mountain air watching the sun rise. The beautiful, glowing stillness fascinated him and it came to him why, when Solomon's Temple had stood at the pinnacle of its glory, this place had induced one of the sons of Korah to write:

Great is the LORD and greatly to be praised
in the city of our God!
His holy mountain, beautiful in elevation,
is the joy of all the earth,
Mount Zion, in the far north,
the city of the great King.
Within her citadels God
has made himself known as a fortress. (Ps. 48:1-3)

Out of sight, to the south and running east-west, stood the accursed Valley of Ben-Hinnom where King Manasseh had practiced child sacrifice, the son of the same Hezekiah who had defied the Assyrians in the name of the God of Israel. Looking close around him, he shuddered as he realized that beneath the long, rough mounds of earth, flattened and smoothed on the top by decades of rain and sun, were enormous burial trenches of those who had not survived the Great Siege:

The joy of our hearts has ceased; our dancing has been turned to mourning. The crown has fallen from our head; woe to us, for we have sinned! For this our heart has become sick, for these things our eyes have grown dim, for Mount Zion which lies desolate; jackals prowl over it. (Lam. 5:15-18)

Turning quickly away and retracing his steps, he thought to himself, "Somewhere near here must be Hezekiah's tunnel taking water from the Gihon Spring." They could see spring water welling up on the south-eastern side but any access was blocked with stones. They looked heavier and deliberately well-packed.

Many in their train were aghast at the destruction. Having been privy to Nebuzaradan's account first hand, Boaz had some vague idea of what to expect, but his fellow wagon-trainers were devastated, despite the fact that they had been warned. Perhaps it was the contrast between the monumental scale of the destruction and the height of their expectation of a return to Jerusalem that brought their spirits crashing down. "How long will it take to bring it back to life?" thought Boaz glumly.

The next few weeks and months brought an answer. Even for a big young man, now hardened by the arduous journey, the work of building even the most modest of houses for shelter, and then clearing the desolate surrounding area of the city, had been exhausting. Local bandits also added to their troubles and slowed their progress. Unblocking the Gihon spring took weeks of arduous work. After the siege, the vast teams of Babylonian slaves and soldiers had shifted massively heavy stones over the entrance to the tunnel. They must have been carted long distances by ox-teams. The Exiles did not have the same manpower but they had oxen whose great strength was employed to good effect once they had worked out how to do it. Finally they cleared the tunnel exit from the south east so the brave could enter the darkness and follow the tunnel to the source of the spring to work out where it went. At least they now had clean water in plentiful supply.

Each night Boaz collapsed into his bed and slept the sleep of the dead. He realized that they had to do much more than rebuild the Temple, or even Jerusalem itself, but reconstruct a country from the ground up. More than that, they had to re-construct a new way of living and thinking. They were Exiles no longer and could not live and think in the way they had been forced to live and think in Babylon. There, survival had been their sole aim, whereas now they were relatively free. To rebuild a city, a nation and a way of obedient living would be the work of a lifetime.

14

THE REBUILDING OF THE TEMPLE

The translucent quality of the Jerusalem dawn light had fascinated Boaz from his first morning. Rising early and wandering up to the Temple Mount to bask in the serenity of the blue-gold glow had become his routine before the exhausting labour of the day ahead. Only later in the year did he discover that Jerusalem's altitude made the winter rain colder than he could have imagined. It even occasionally turned to snow. The habit of daily prayer also came easily to him as each morning he pondered on the great events of which he had been so much a part. The brilliant blue clarity of the air by day merged into darkly stained satin at night in which a huge sweep of stars glittered like a vast swathe of tiny diamonds. 'Diamond fire-dust' someone had called it. Boaz had never seen a diamond but he could attest that the Jerusalem night sky had a milky, sparkling, phosphorescence streaked with colour that he had never seen in Babylon where it had been masked by the haze from fires, kilns and river mist. The vast skies of Jerusalem by day and night left him over-awed. "We are so small and the sky is so huge. Was it these same skies that Father Abraham observed when he was promised 'Look toward heaven, and number the stars, if you are able to number them. So shall your off-spring be.'?[59] Did King David see the same standing on this Mount?" he wondered. "Could they have conceived what their children have experienced, from great wealth to anguished poverty and exile? Now Zion is a wasteland and Abraham's off-spring are scattered in exile. His wealth had lain in his great herds while David's gold, silver and bronze, left to Solomon for the Temple decoration, had been stripped, melted and carried off."

Huge herds he had seen on his travels but neither silver nor gold in great quantities and certainly no diamonds. In his childhood some of his people had talked quietly of the great gold and silver vessels of Solomon's Temple that had been taken to Babylon at the second deportation, but these had then been beyond his boyish conception. It had been assumed that they had been lost and melted down, but then, on that special night with Boaz and the elders of Judah many years ago, Nebuzaradan had told them a piece of news that had arrested their ears. The Temple vessels had not been arbitrarily scattered, as they had supposed. Under Nebuchadnezzar's orders, they had been placed in various pagan temples and were safe. It was from these that the vain and empty-headed Belshazzar had wished to drink on the night of his feast before his deposition.

After the edict issued in the previous year, these vessels had been placed in the charge of Mithredath the treasurer, who had counted them with great ceremony. The vessels of gold and of silver had numbered 5,400. These vessels had subsequently travelled with Zerubbabel, Jeshua (the High Priest) son of Jozadak, and many of the leading families who finally reached Jerusalem some time after Boaz' vanguard had established itself. Many other groups had travelled back to the ruins of their ancestral homes in the surrounding towns of Judah. To their dismay, they discovered first-hand the extent of Nebuchadnezzar's fury and how complete the Babylonian devastation of Judah had been. Their towns were in ruins and each ancestral field and vineyard was an overgrown wilderness whose restoration would require years of intensive and back breaking labour.

59   Gen. 15:5.

During that first year, the returning Exiles gathered together in Jerusalem. Jeshua the son of Jozadak, his fellow priests, Zerubbabel the son of Shealtiel arose, and together rebuilt the altar of the God of Israel, to offer burnt offerings on it, as it is written in the Law of Moses. They set the altar in its place and they offered burnt offerings morning and evening using the recovered Temple vessels. In size, the reclaimed territory of Judah measured an insignificant area of about 25 by 30 miles. The ruination of the land by the Babylonian army, who had littered it with stones, and their destruction of the woodland and forests, had meant that the land had become un-farmable in its present derelict state. Few people lived in or around the city but of those that did, some had Judahite ancestry who had been escapees from the Babylonian army at the Great Siege. Others were the descendants of migrants from the tribes settled by the Assyrians further north. A subsistence life scratched from the soil had been their lot. The arrival of Boaz' vanguard had been met by puzzlement, even mild amusement, but as more were being added to their number each month, and the entity spread, so the hostility grew as they realised that the Judahites were there to stay.

The writ of a far-off Persian king ran ineffectually in such far-off provinces. Legal declarations with royal seals meant little if there was nobody to enforce them. The local government officials and their soldiery dragged their feet and did nothing to help. It was clear that the Exiles were on their own. It therefore became necessary to set a continuous guard around Jerusalem and its surrounding towns. It was more difficult to guard those who worked in the outer fields and vineyards, particularly the shepherds in the surrounding hills. These armed themselves against both wolves and lions as well as bandits. It was especially necessary to guard the Temple area and particularly the altar. If that could be destroyed and the safety of the Temple area made untenable then their attempt to rebuild their country would fail. Boaz himself took part in many a local defensive skirmish, but he and his fellow Judahites had been too well drilled by their instructors to encounter serious difficulties. Those weeks of rigorous training learning how to handle spear and sword had been well-spent. Yet

again he blessed Baltazar's foresight but he also began to understand
why he had suffered Adar's fury a few months before. They really were
on their own. Their enthusiasm was still strong, but what of next year,
the year after and then ten years from now? Could they continue to
patrol the Temple Mount forever, never letting down their guard?
Would their enterprise put down roots or wither on the vine through
lack of fortitude and understanding? They had to recover their identity as the people of God, obedient to his commands, in a world that
was at best dismissive and at worst downright hostile. It came to him
that as an official scribe it was up to him to teach and lead by example.
Never before had he felt the weight of the world on his shoulders.

   While the altar had been built, the foundation of the new
Temple had not been laid. For this they needed seasoned wood to lay
between courses of stone. The forests around Judah and Israel had
been destroyed during the Great Siege and had not recovered. It was
possible they never would. To acquire locally the necessary size of
tree was impossible, so they did a deal with the people of the cities of
Sidon and Tyre to the north in Lebanon. In exchange for grain, wine,
and olive oil, logs of cedars of Lebanon were floated down the coast
to Joppa,[60] as in the days of Solomon, and hauled up to Jerusalem by
ox-train. In the second year after their coming to Jerusalem, in the
second month, Zerubbabel the son of Shealtiel and Jeshua the son of
Jozadak made a beginning on the foundation, together with the rest
of their kinsmen, the priests and the Levites and all who had come
to Jerusalem from the captivity. They appointed the Levites, from
twenty years old and upward, to supervise the work. Only those who
could prove their Levitical descent worked directly on the foundation
of the Temple itself. As with many of his orphaned kind, although
informed that his father had been a Levite, Boaz could not trace his
lineage properly.

   A generation before, the Babylonian teams of slaves and soldiers
had not only pulled down the walls of the old City of David, they had
even made attempts to destroy the individual big chisel-shaped stones
to make them unusable again. Some of these had crushed edges but

60   Ezra 3:8-10.

were still re-usable. Others were broken or cracked right through but the pieces could be re-shaped by masons into smaller stones fit for a new wall. Since boyhood, Boaz had always had a fascination with walls, having spent hours staring at the great walls of Babylon. This fascination had finally come home to roost, for the task assigned to him was to lead the re-building of the city walls. Their first task was to rescue as many of the broken and discarded stones as possible. They would not have the chisel-shaped elegance of their forbears, but they could still be strong and serviceable if built properly. Everyone was assigned a manual task and although Boaz was a scholar, and by now a scribe, his size, strength and character made him suitable to lead this laborious and exhausting work. His team of men attacked the task with energy, for they realised that the future safety of their city depended on them. A city without walls was open to constant attack and plundering raids.[61]

Slowly, very slowly, they cleared away the brambles and weeds to expose the old foundations of the city walls and hauled rescued stones from the vast piles littering the sides of the Kidron Valley. Some of the old foundations had even been dug up but large sections remained in place. Even more slowly they began to lay new courses on the remaining foundations and seal the gaps in newly cleared trenches. After months of exhausting work an outline of the old city began to appear at about ankle or knee height. It was only a start and it would take many decades to finish, but the outline gave them hope. Their aim was to build walls to shoulder or head height which would make them safe from marauding bands of cavalry even though they would still be

---

61   The book of Nehemiah (1:3) records that his journey from Persia to Jerusalem was caused by the distressing news he had received in a letter from Jerusalem that said "The remnant there in the province who have survived the Exile is in great trouble and shame. The wall of Jerusalem is broken down, and its gates are destroyed by fire." This event took place around 445 BCE, seventy one years after the second Temple was inaugurated in 516 BCE. Given the evident distress of Nehemiah and his correspondent, it is not psychologically credible that the wall referred to in the letter was the original city wall destroyed by the Babylonian army in 587 BCE. After all, it would have had to have lain undisturbed in ruins for 142 years. The most likely explanation is that the city wall had been rebuilt in that 71 year gap, although who built it has never been discovered. The identity of the attackers who reduced it once more to rubble is also unknown. In the story, this wall is the one begun by Boaz, coincident with the laying of the Temple foundations about ninety years before, but whose construction was halted by the edict of Darius the King.

scalable by men on foot. Together with viable gates, this would make Jerusalem a safer walled city again.

After the builders laid the foundation of the Temple, the priests in their vestments came forward with trumpets, and the Levites, the sons of Asaph, with cymbals, to praise the God of Israel, according to the directions of David, King of Israel.

Far-flung empires of all types employ officials who specialize in obstruction, usually in corrupt connivance with other local power-brokers. Persian-ruled Jerusalem was no exception.

Standing on the steps leading up to the platform that was intended to be the foundation of the new Temple, Boaz could not help but let his disappointment show in the sag of his shoulders. That very day an edict had come through from the King of Persia who had declared that the building work on the new Temple and the walls must cease. They had begun construction with such faith and energy and had finished the foundations with much rejoicing. They were immensely deflated when it turned out that Rehum the commander of the official local forces, Shimshai the scribe and others had written a letter of accusation against those, including himself, who had returned from Babylon. Rehum and Shimshai had been alarmed to see the altar, the platform for the new Temple and the outline of the city walls, all of which demonstrated the Judahite determination to restore Jerusalem as a centre of worship and life. The charges were absurd, of course, and had massively exaggerated Jerusalem's rebellious history, but distant royal court officials were always willing to listen to those who paid the largest bribe or who had the most influence. The King had listened and issued a decree ordering them to cease their building.

In that moment he reminded himself that Jeremiah had begun his prophesying on the steps of Solomon's Temple, now long disappeared in dust and ashes. In his reverie he mused on the last three tumultuous years, including the fourteen years that had elapsed since that fateful evening meeting with Baruch and Nebuzaradan. Although that night remained the defining moment of his life, it had been the scolding Adar had given him for naivety on the journey that had forcibly caused him to mature from a boy into a man. The man in him would not let this setback discourage him. The King's decree was just a setback, nothing more. Of this he was sure. In the end they would prevail.

Twenty more years passed. The rebuilding of the Temple and the issue of the walls still remained in a legal deep freeze by royal decree. The number of returning Exiles had increased and, while the local government officials had reluctantly accepted that they were there to stay, they still looked upon the fledgling entity with suspicion. Boaz had worked away the years as both a builder and a scribe. In spring and summer he continued his habit of rising early and stealing the dawn, as he thought of it, by watching the sun rise over the eastern mount[62] but each day, as he looked up at the steps of the unfinished Temple and the walls, he felt a sense of deep regret. Nevertheless, he also had a lingering sense that they would ultimately prevail.

In the second year of Darius[63] the King, Haggai the prophet spoke the following words to Zerubbabel the son of Shealtiel,[64] governor of Judah, and to Joshua the son of Jehozadak, the high priest:

Thus says the LORD of hosts: These people say the time has not yet come to rebuild the house of the LORD. ... Consider your ways. Go up to the hills and bring wood and build the house, that I may take pleasure in it and that I may be glorified, says the LORD. You looked for much, and behold, it came to little. And when you brought it home, I blew it away. Why? Because

---

62 Later known as the Mount of Olives.

63 Darius 1st was king during the period 519 – 465 BCE.

64 Zerubbabel, the son of Shealtiel, was the grandson of King Jehoiachin (Jeconiah) who had been taken to Babylon in the second deportation in 597 BCE.

of my house that lies in ruins, while each of you busies himself
with his own house. (Hag. 1:2 and 7-9)

It was true that the people had looked to their own houses first.
Perhaps it was natural that they looked to their own security and com-
fort in difficult times while they established the entity, but it meant
that they had taken their eyes off the main task. Haggai's words woke
the people up, so they obeyed and began to build. Hardly surprisingly,
Tattenai the governor of the province[65] and his associates immediately challenged them and asked: "Who gave you a decree to build this
house and to finish this structure?" They answered that their permission came through the original decree of Cyrus the Great. This answer
could have been given many years ago but they had not pursued it.
For this laxity the community felt guilty but having woken up they
were determined to proceed. When their answer was forwarded to
Darius the King, a search was made for this decree which was duly
found stored in the citadel in Ecbatana in the province of Media. Not
only did this decree give them permission to rebuild, it also said that
the gold and silver vessels of the house of God, removed from the
original Temple, should be returned as indeed they had been. In addition, Darius the King forbade the local officials to interfere; even better, they were ordered to provide resources.
    It was a reversal so complete that Boaz' head had spun.

    On the evening of the day of the inauguration of the new Temple
he again stood on its steps, just before the Evening Sacrifice, and
thought back to that night when Baruch had recounted all the events
of that momentous day when Jeremiah had uttered his first prophecy
on the steps of Solomon's Temple. The memory of the stinging words
rang in his mind:

---

65   The Persian name for the province was 'Beyond the River'.

What wrong did your fathers find in me that they went far
from me, and went after worthlessness, and became worthless?
(Jer. 2:4)

"How much grief and blood has been shed between then and now?"
he wondered. He offered a quiet prayer of humble gratitude for having had the chance to contribute to this new start. He looked up at
the new Temple, a modest structure at best, and wondered whether
Jeremiah the prophet and Baruch the scribe would have approved of
it? By now Boaz was no longer the innocent, naive, dreamy boy of
that first night, but a strong, heavily-muscled, weather-beaten man
in his fifties with a family. His early promise as a scholar had not been
wasted but now stood alongside his early years of labour on the walls
and then on the city buildings and the land. Indeed, he was widely
respected not only for his wisdom as a scribe but also for his great
height and strength. People called him 'Boaz the Pillar', in allusion to
the eighteen cubit northern pillar in the porch of Solomon's Temple.
The writings of Jeremiah, now committed to memory, had become
so much a part of him that passages often floated into his mind as
he worked:

The people who survived the sword
found grace in the wilderness;
when Israel sought for rest,
the LORD appeared to him from far away.
I have loved you with an everlasting love;
therefore I have continued my faithfulness to you.
Again I will build you, and you shall be built,
O virgin Israel! (Jer. 31:2-4)

His old teacher Itamar, long since dead, had been right: the love of
the LORD is indeed everlasting. The new Temple was a long way from
the first gold-encrusted edifice, nor had the Presence appeared in
the Most Holy Place as in Solomon's days, but it was a more humble
beginning for a new age. It had been a long journey from Babylon but

there would be no return to Egypt this time. The heavily emphasized words of his teacher Itamar came back to him from more than thirty years ago; "*Remember, our God does not carry passengers when taking his people on a journey.*" It had begun as a journey of return and restoration, but it had ended as a journey of the heart. The second verse of the Shema had become real to him:

> And you shall love the LORD your God with all your heart and with all your soul and with all your strength. (Deut. 6-5)

Judah was no longer an independent kingdom of David's line but was now a tiny, obscure, provincial entity of returned Exiles sitting on the edge of the western sea and ruled by officials of the huge Persian Empire. During his physically demanding work, first on the fledgling city walls and then the city buildings, and his mentally demanding studies of the writings of the old Hebrew prophets, he had come to realize that Jerusalem stood for more than just a physical city built of stone:

> Arise, shine, for your light has come,
> and the glory of the LORD has risen upon you.
> For behold, darkness shall cover the earth,
> and thick darkness the peoples;
> but the LORD will arise upon you,
> and his glory will be seen upon you.
> And nations shall come to your light,
> and kings to the brightness of your rising. (Is. 60:1-3)

"The foundation of these little walls standing at my feet I built with my own hands," he thought. "I know their strengths and their weak points. It has to have a deeper meaning."

> Walk about Zion, go around her,
> number her towers,
> consider well her ramparts,

go through her citadels,
that you may tell the next generation
that this is God, our God forever and ever.
He will guide us forever. (Ps. 48:12-14)

He constantly urged his people to understand that a true return to Jerusalem was more than just a physical journey to the city but had to be a return to the LORD in heart, soul and mind. The true Jerusalem is a place built by God himself, where he will dwell forever in a home for his people: "He has torn us, but he will heal us; he has struck us down, but he will bind us up. After two days he will revive us, but on the third day he will raise us up, that we may live before him."[66] He repeatedly insisted that they had to live as they professed to believe. "It is not enough to donate your sacrifices and pay money as if this excused evil living. If you profess belief in our God then live obediently before the One whose eyes are always upon us. Remember the first commandment?"

You shall not make for yourself a carved image, or any like-ness of anything that is in heaven above, or that is in the earth beneath, or that is in the water under the earth. You shall not bow down to them or serve them, for I the LORD your God am a jealous God ... (Ex. 20:4-5)

"Some of you have begun to live the way the Canaanites lived, as our fathers did before the Exile, who lost their way over this form of dis-obedience. Remember Moses who fasted for forty days and nights on Sinai after the Golden Calf? Let us press on to know the LORD, his going out is sure as the dawn. He will come to us as the showers, as the spring rains that water the earth." He spoke with force often on this topic. Indeed, patience with them and with himself was a character attribute he had had to learn the hard way over the decades.

---

66 Hosea 3:1-3.

Old men often dwell on the past but he found himself dwelling more on the future. His studies of Jeremiah's writings had shown him that not all the prophet's writings had been about warnings of disaster that had so agonizingly come to pass. The passages about future restoration had concentrated his mind on a more glorious future.

"Behold, I will restore the fortunes of the tents of Jacob
and have compassion on his dwellings;
the city shall be rebuilt on its mound,
and the palace shall stand where it used to be.
Out of them shall come songs of thanksgiving,
and the voices of those who celebrate.
I will multiply them, and they shall not be few;
I will make them honoured, and they shall not be small.
Their children shall be as they were of old,
and their congregation shall be established before me,
and I will punish all who oppress them.
Their Prince shall be one of themselves;
their ruler shall come out from their midst;
I will make him draw near, and he shall approach me,
for who would dare of himself to approach me?"
declares the LORD.
"And you shall be my people, and I will be your God."
(Jer. 30:18-22)

His mind turned over the likelihood of ever seeing the day of this new Prince. Given his age, no, it was not likely, but then he had no pretensions to greatness or glory. To serve and wait upon the Lord God of Israel in simple faith of sins forgiven and a home beyond the grave was enough. To wait for that he had all the patience in the world.

ALPHABETICAL GLOSSARY OF NAMES AND PLACES (ALL DATES BCE)

A: *Adar*; fictional Judahite soldier, scout and leader of the vanguard on the return to Jerusalem.

Amon; son of Manasseh, King of Judah (c. 642-640).

Ammon; a nation located in modern Jordan from which the city of Amman derives its name.

Arioch; Captain of the Babylonian Royal Guard sometime prior to Nebuzaradan.

Ashpenaz; in charge of Daniel and his young companions Shadrach (Hananiah), Meshach (Mishael) and Abednego (Azariah) at the court of Nebuchadnezzar.

Ashur; a city in the Assyrian Empire and once its capital.

Assurbanipal; King of Assyria (c. 669-631).

B: *Baltazar*; fictional great grandson of Nebuzaradan.

        Baruch; Jeremiah's secretary and friend. According to Jer. 32:12 and 2 Chron. 34:8, Baruch's grandfather, Maaseiah, had been governor of Jerusalem.

        Beth-Shan, an ancient Israelite city south of the Sea of Kinneret (Galilee).

        Boaz; (a fictional character).

C: *Cyrus the Great*; King of Anshan, Persia, Media and Babylon (c. 598-530).

D: *Damascus*; ancient capital city in Syria.

        Daniel; a young Judahite, who was deported in the first wave from Jerusalem to Babylon: his Babylonian given name was Belteshazzar. He ultimately became a high Government official in the Babylonian and Persian Empires.

        Darius 1st; King of Persia (519-465).

        David; first full King of all Israel (1010-970).

        Deborah; matron of the Residence (a fictional character).

E: *Ebed-Melech*; a eunuch in the court of King Zedekiah who pleaded for the life of Jeremiah and subsequently pulled him out of the muddy cistern.

        Ecbatana; a city in Media, and part of the Persian Empire.

        Elam; ancient Empire located in modern Iran on the north side of the Persian Gulf.

        Eleazar; Chief Judahite scribe in the city of Babylon (a fictional character).

G: *Gedaliah*; appointed Governor of Judah and Jerusalem by Nebuzaradan after the Great Siege and third deportation in 587/6, but murdered by local guerillas.

Gihon Spring; an intermittent siphon-spring in the Kidron Valley that supplied water to Jerusalem, which it still does to this day. In the 8th century BCE, King Hezekiah had a tunnel cut in the rock to channel the water back into the city.

Gobryas; the conqueror of Babylon under Cyrus.

H: *Haggai*; a Hebrew prophet of the late 6th century BCE.

Hananiah; a false prophet mentioned in Jer. 28.

Hazor; a great fortress town in Northern Israel.

Hezekiah; King of Judah (739-687).

Hilkiah; a priest and father of Jeremiah.

Hilkiah; the High Priest at the time of King Josiah.

Hophra; Egyptian Pharaoh (589-570).

Hulda; the prophetess and wife of Shallum who lived in Jerusalem at the time of King Josiah.

I: *Isaiah*; 8th century BCE Judahite prophet.

Ishmael; leader of a guerrilla band who, at the behest of the Ammonite King, murdered the appointed Governor, Gedaliah, after the Siege.

Itamar; Boaz' teacher (a fictional character).

J: *Jehoiakim (Eliakim)*; King of Judah (609-598).

Jehoiachin (Jeconiah or Coniah); King of Judah (3 months in 597), deported to Babylon.

Jehoahaz (Shallum); King of Judah: reigned for 3 months in 609. Deported to Egypt by Pharaoh Necho.

Jeremiah; the Prophet (640-c.570).

Jeshua; the High Priest, son of Jozadak.

Johanan; leader of the Judahite remnant after Gedaliah's murder, who led them down to Egypt.

Josiah; King of Judah (640-609).

Joseph; fictional cover name for Baruch.

Jozadak; the High Priest during the Exile.

K: *Kinneret or Gennesaret*; other names for the Sea of Galilee.

M: *Manasseh*; King of Judah (697-642).

Marduk, master-god in the Babylonian pantheon.

Mithradath; treasurer in the court of King Cyrus, who counted out the Temple vessels on their return.

Moab; a nation located directly east of the Dead Sea, south of Ammon.

Mordecai; fictional secretary of Teresh the Persian merchant.

N: *Nabopolassar*; (658-605), governor and then King of Babylon, and father of Nebuchadnezzar;

Nebo, scribe to the Babylonian gods.

Nebuchadnezzar; King of the Babylonian Empire (605-562).

Nebuzaradan; Captain of the Babylonian Royal Guard.

Nineveh; capital of the Assyrian Empire.

Necho; Egyptian Pharaoh (610-595/4)

R: *Riblah*; a city in the land of Hamath on the Lebanese-Syrian border.

Rehum and Shimshai; officials of the Persian government in Jerusalem.

Ruth; the Moabitess, great grandmother of King David.

S: *Samaria*; capital city of the Northern Kingdom of Israel after the split with Judah, destroyed by the Assyrians 722.

Sennacherib; King of Assyria (705-681).

Shemaiah; a false prophet mentioned in Jer. 29.

Shaphan; secretary to King Josiah.

Solomon; son of David, builder of the first Jerusalem Temple, and King of all Israel (970-930).

Susa; an ancient city of the Elamite and Persian Empires.

T: *Tadmor*; ancient city in Syria, and renamed Palmyra in Roman times.

Tahpanhes; the Egyptian city where Jeremiah died. Tahpanhes, Migdol and Memphis all contained significant idolatrous Judahite communities.

Tattenai; Governor of the Province of 'Beyond the River' (Euphrates), the Persian name for the area that included the old lands of Judah and Israel.

Teresh; a fictional Persian merchant.

Tyre; an ancient city of the Phoenicians located on the coast of Lebanon.

V: *Valley of Ben-Hinnom (Gehenna)*; a place just outside of the city
       of Jerusalem where some of the kings of Judah, and others,
       sacrificed their children by fire

Z: *Zedekiah (Mattaniah)*; King of Judah (597-587/6).

       Zephaniah; 7th century Hebrew prophet.

       Zerubbabel; the Babylonian name of a Prince of the Royal
       Family of Judah, which means 'seed of Babylon'.

ABOUT THE AUTHOR

The author was born in 1949 in Manchester, UK. He was an undergraduate at the University of Birmingham (1967-70) and then received his PhD in Mathematics from the University of Manchester in 1973. He has lived in London since 1980 when he joined the Mathematics Department of Imperial College London. He was promoted to full Professor in 1990 and served as a Consul (2007-10). Consuls are senior Faculty who are elected to manage issues such as the academic promotions process, academic standards in appointments and the award of prizes. He is now an Emeritus Professor of Applied Mathematics.

His area of research is in the theory of turbulent fluid flows, with current collaborators in the United Kingdom, United States, France, and India. He has published more than 125 research papers and co-authored two books, *Applied Analysis of the Navier-Stokes Equations* (Cambridge University Press, 1995) and *Nonlinear Waves and Solitons* (Academic Press, 1983), and is the author of *Science and the Knowledge of God* (Lampion Press, 2015). He and his wife Sheila are members of Duke Street Church, Richmond, in southwest London.